The Original Plan

A novel by Robert Sefer

The Original Plan

ISBN: 9781973474111

Published in the United States of America

Written in Hungarian

(Original title: *Az eredeti terv*)

Translated into English by

Leonora Franciskovity

Proofreader

Zoltan Brasnyo

Book cover

Pixabay

In memory of
my grandmother

– 1 –

After I had died, for a very short period of time, I was not sure what had happened to me. Of course, I was suspecting it, but still, the first thought that came to my mind was that I was only dreaming. I made this wrong conclusion primarily due to the fact that death came to me while I was sleeping.

But there was something else, too, that made me think that my journey to the afterlife was only a dream: I could *see* with my eyes closed and I could *hear* the sounds not with my ears, but so to speak, they were coming from the inside. This experience was undoubtedly similar to the world of dreams, thus, I think it is not surprising at all that I was a little confused at the very beginning.

Otherwise, seeing without eyes and hearing without ears is not only a phenomenon that is typical for our dreams: we can meet it in our everyday life very often. For example, when reading a book, the sentences sound in our inner voice, the described locations, living beings and objects are seen as though they would be really there. This ability is an integral part of our lives, however, we will really use it after our deaths...

I realized this a few seconds later when I began remembering facts which suggested that I was not dreaming. Obviously, the best argument about my death was that I was lying in the hospital as a patient in end-stage cancer. I knew I was going to die. And as time passed, I was more aware that this was what had happened to me.

But suppose that I did not die in the hospital waiting for, or to be more precise, calling for death to release me, but rather I died suddenly in a car accident, for instance. Well, even then I would not have believed for long that I was dreaming, because everything that I could see and hear was more realistic than any of dreams I had had by then!

As we know, the majority of our dreams are meaningless, the pictures are often not sharp, the words and the sentences usually do not make any sense. But to my biggest surprise, at that very moment, I could see, hear and understand everything clearly! Everyone would recognize this difference, regardless whether he suffered a lot or died suddenly. At least, it would just take them a little longer to figure it out.

And there was one more thing that convinced me that this could not have been just a dream. Those who had a near-death experience claimed that their life had flashed before their eyes. They said that they saw the totality of their life history in chronological sequence, rapidly in a few seconds, in extreme detail. I had always believed these accounts, despite lacking such an experience. What is more: I have not had such an experience not even after my death! My life review was not like that at all. I saw many strange things...

For instance, the film began with a childhood memory that I had not even been able to recall while I was alive. I saw my parents who were as young as they were in their wedding photos. Even my mother's father was there, who had died before my first birthday. I never had a memory of him while I was alive. I saw him only in photos and I "knew" him only from stories. But at that moment, he was sitting on the couch in front of me and he was smiling. He grabbed a glass of juice and he began talking with my very young parents and grandmother.

It was fascinating that I could understand every word even though it was obvious that these memories were from my infancy. I was confused and I did not understand what was happening, so I began thinking.

I already rejected the idea that what I saw was only a dream. But what was it then? My life review? Everyone said that it lasted only for a second, but what I saw did not consist of rapidly changing short scenes—it happened in real time! So, I came to a conclusion that what was happening to me could be neither a dream nor the review of my life. It was similar to both, but there were much more differences.

That was the moment when I began to realize that something has changed in my life forever. It was not a problem for me to accept the fact of my death and that probably I could by no means go back to my body. But then, who knows why, I did not reject the possibility that I would wake up in my hospital bed realizing that I was only dreaming or hallucinating due to strong painkillers. Not to be misunderstood: I did not desire it. It was the most terrible scenario that I could imagine. I did not want at all to wake up in the hospital and continue suffering...

After this I stopped thinking for a while and I paid attention to the scene from my infancy. The TV was on and the news from the time of my birth could be heard in the background. This made me ask myself a few questions.

What is happening to me? Am I reliving my very first day in the world? Or at least, the day when I was with my closest family for the first time? Is this how we meet our loved ones after death?

I had plenty of questions, but I was certain in one thing: it was very moving. It was so heartwarming to see everyone around me with love and joy. But since I knew that my parents and grandparents loved me, I did not understand why I had to see all these things...

And when this old—but for me a very new—memory began to be a little boring, the scene changed in a minute: now I was sitting on the carpet so familiar from my childhood, on the floor beside a Christmas tree and I was just opening a present. I must have been around three. I wanted to look around, but I had to realize very soon that I could move neither my hands nor my head. I could see everything only from the original perspective.

After approximately an hour, when I had seen around the twentieth scene as well, it became obvious to me that I was watching the happiest and the most beautiful moments of my life. And at this point I even enjoyed the show, because I remembered the things presented. It was amazing how accurate the scenes were! In our dreams the sounds and the pictures are not at all so realistic...

Suddenly, it occurred to me that I was probably going to relive my first kiss as well, and this made me very excited. I was waiting for that scene so much that I did not even realize I had almost completely accepted the fact of my death. Now it was my first vacation in the film, but I could not guess how much time I had till the kiss. Of course, I knew exactly when, where and with whom it had happened. I just did not know how many joyful moments and memories I was going to see until then.

And because re-experiencing my first meeting with the salty water could not grab my attention entirely, I began questioning again.

Does this happen to everyone after death? Does everyone see the best moments of their life? Is this the heaven thought by so many people to exist? I have to tell that the feeling was undoubtedly heavenly. To relive all the cheerful memories and to meet our loved ones, the people who were important in our life, this really is heaven! But what is then hell? The worst parts of our lives are repeated? Well, it is hard to imagine something more hellish than to relive everything that caused us pain and made us suffer—with the torturing slowness of real time.

The film was still dealing with the nicest memories of my first seaside vacation, when it came to my mind:

What will happen when there are no more memories? Yes, I knew I had not seen even my first kiss, but I also knew that sooner or later I would arrive at the end of my life, and from that period I did not have so many nice memories… So, when does our life review end? Does it end with our last joyful memory? Or does it last until our death? And what if it does not end there either? I must say, the thought that I might have to watch my funeral made me very sad. I did not want to see my loved ones grieve.

But instead of asking new questions I decided that I had better wait until the end. After all, I could not do anything else. I could not even move my head, so I was forced to pay attention to my experience. Of course, from time to time I tried to move my head, or at least my eyes or my hands, but it was all in vain. I could not even close my eyes, which after all did not surprise me, because by then I knew for sure that I was not alive. In other words: I was not in my body anymore. This was very bizarre and a little bit frightening, but most of all it was a pleasant feeling as well. I was free and light, so to say, weightless.

The film still did not even reach my first kiss, when the picture suddenly disappeared! The beach was nowhere, the sentence of my mother, who was oiling my back, was interrupted. Not between two words but in the middle of a single one. There was silence and total darkness. I tried to open my eyes, but nothing happened.

After a few seconds I heard noises. First something that was like the beeping of a hospital machine, and then I heard a human voice as well:

"We made it! Here is our next guest!"

– 2 –

I realized an enormous change even before I opened my eyes: I was not weightless anymore.

Six months ago, the medical results showed that I had contracted a deadly disease. At the final stage of the degradation I felt my body to be very heavy and painful. I could hardly bear it, even though I was very thin due to my weight loss. However, in the past hour, while I was watching my life review, I did not feel my body. I could not even control it, since there was nothing to control either. But now, I felt exactly the same as I had before my illness, when I was healthy.

I opened my eyes slowly. First, I saw two pairs of shoes on the floor, and when I looked up, I saw the silhouettes of two persons. I could not see them clearly, but I could hear them:

"Do you think we will be able to communicate with him?"

"I hope so."

Even though I knew exactly that I was dead, my first

thought was that I was back to the hospital for reanimation. But it became obvious very quickly that I was not lying on a bed but sitting on a chair. And when I looked at myself—I could move my head again—I realized that I was a child!

When I could open my eyes widely, everything became clearer. I felt like I had just woken up after a ten-hour sleep.

The room looked like a laboratory. By my side there were five children sitting on similar chairs. They all looked the same. They were motionless, their eyes closed and heads turned down, instruments and wires all around them. I was sure that I looked the same as they did, and that we might have been taking part in a scientific experiment or something like that.

What surprised me was that the people in front of me were also children. They both had short, black hair. One of them had white skin, the other was something darker. They were wearing silver-blue clothes, and their faces appeared Asiatic. They were not exactly the same, like the five people by my side, but they were very similar to each other.

In order to make this story more clear—and because they did not introduce themselves—I gave them names. Yin was the one who had a little darker complexion, and I named the other one Yang.

Yang left the room immediately, but Yin stayed with me. He leaned towards me and looked directly into my eyes. And then something strange happened. Despite my wish, I heard my inner voice!

"Welcome! I hope you are all right. I believe you will easily adjust to this body since you have already lived in a similar one."

I think it is needless to say how strange it was to hear the thoughts of someone else in my head! I was frightened, because I had a feeling that somebody else was directing my thoughts. I was so shocked that I could only say this to Yin:

"Are *you* talking to me?" and my astonishment became even bigger, because I was speaking in a high, childlike voice. It was not similar at all to my deep tone that I used to know my entire lifetime.

I could hear my inner voice again, however, Yin did not pronounce a word, his lips were not moving. He was just looking at me:

"Yes, it is me who is talking to you. I see that you are not familiar with this type of communication yet..."

And then I think I interrupted him, because I wanted to know something:

"I am dead, aren't I?"

"Yes, you are," answered Yin immediately, and he showed no pity.

"Where am I then? And who are you?" I was still surprised by my new voice.

"I am afraid that you would not understand the answer, because it can include concepts that are still unknown to you. This kind of communication works like this: a concept becomes a thought in my head and I send it to you, but you will understand it only if you are familiar with the meaning of that concept. Is this clear so far?"

"Of course," I answered, and for the first time I was not communicating by using my speech organs but by telepathy. It was very surprising that I could learn so easily to use this kind of communication.

"I am glad for you!" said Yin. "But now I do not understand why you were so confused when I talked to you in this way."

"Well..." I hesitated, "I have never met anyone who knows how to use telepathy. You are the first. It is true that I have heard that some people know how to communicate by means of this language, but..."

"Telepathy is not a language," Yin interrupted me. "There is a relation between language and thoughts, but it is insignificant. The spoken language is a communication used only in the material world. In order to realize it, materials, or to be more precise: organs of speech, sound waves that transmit air molecules and organs of hearing are needed. However, thoughts are non-material. It is much better to communicate by means of them, because they are represented as concepts and images. Language is only a weak attempt to express our thoughts in words. Thus, we use a more advanced communication instead of the material world's spoken language. We send images and concepts to each other. Do you understand this?"

"I understand," I answered.

"Great! According to this, your civilization belongs to advanced ones. We have not had such a meeting for a long time. We have been looking forward to it!"

"And where am I exactly?" I repeated my previous question, although I could have guessed the answer after *civilization* and *meeting* had been mentioned.

"You are on another planet. The same people live here as on the planet where you died a few hours ago."

"I understand you. I am now on another planet in a body of another man," I summed up.

"Yes. I am glad that we can so easily understand each other! It is a rare and an appreciated moment when we meet someone from an advanced civilization."

"And what about my original body? Can I go back into it again?" I asked, even though I knew the answer would be negative.

"Yes, you are right. You cannot go back into your body or to your planet," said Yin.

What to say... It was very surprising that Yin heard everything that was going on in my head: not only the questions that I asked him but also the answers that I expected. I understood that in this way I could not lie to him—which I, of course, did not want to do either—but if this was the case in reverse, then Yin was also always telling the truth to me. I liked this situation very much. After all, people can say anything, but in their heads there is only one truth, said or unsaid. So, I asked him immediately:

"What is happening with the others? With my deceased loved ones and friends. Did they also get a new body?"

"No, they did not."

"But can I see them?"

"Probably yes, but not here."

"Does not everyone come here after death?" I was surprised.

"No one has to get here. This is not the final destination."

"Then? What is it?" I asked and I became very confused.

"We do not know for sure," answered Yin. "We make this experiment in order to get the answer to this question."

"But what kind of experiment is this? And will I ever get to the place where everyone else gets after death?"

"Of course you will. Everyone gets there."

"But I am not there! You have just said that!" I was very frustrated, because I felt like something was taken from me, something that I was supposed to have.

Yin probably felt this anxiety, because he said the following:

"Don't worry. You can be sure that you will reach the afterlife. We can only slow down this process, but in the end you will get to that place. You have no reason to be angry. Your soul will leave this temporary body, and you will continue your journey just where you have stopped."

"When will it happen?"

"When we begin the experiment."

"And when will that be?"

"In half an hour at most," answered Yin. "Our plan is to send you to the afterlife, and later on, when you have arrived and you have learnt everything about it, we would like to bring you back. We are very curious about that place..."

I was very quiet. Yin continued:

"We have learnt quite a lot about the Universe and life. I can even say that we know everything. But we still do not have the answer to one question: what is waiting for us after death? Of course, we have some theories..."

"How interesting..." I said. "We also have theories, but I think that we do not know about the Universe as much as you do..."

"That is not a problem. While we are preparing for the experiment, we would like to talk with you and to get information about your civilization."

"All right," I said. "However, I am not sure that I can tell you anything new or useful..."

"Well... It is true that every civilization is similar in some way, but there are small differences as well. You can be sure that our conversation will not be in vain."

"Why don't you just download my memories? Wouldn't it be easier?"

"We cannot do that."

"But as I see it, you are members of a very advanced civilization," I remarked.

"It is not that we are not able to do it. We cannot reach your memories only because this is not your original body. However, it is not the case with the people who are born on our planet."

"I see..."

"Anyway, I think that we are only a few thousand years ahead of you. I would like to know at which level of advancement you are at this moment," Yin said, and then he gave me a glass of water-like liquid. "Drink this."

"What is this?" I asked.

"Just drink it. This is what keeps us alive. And as long as you are in this body, you will need it," he answered and headed towards the door, but I could still hear his thoughts in my inner voice. "I will be back in a minute!"

When I drank that water-like liquid, I began thinking.

I still cannot decide whether I was happy or sad then. I had good reasons to be happy, because I met members of a civilization which was ahead of us. These people knew the answers to such questions that intrigued me and my civilization long ago. So, I was glad that I could learn so many things. But the possibility that I could not understand their answers made me sad. And even if I understood everything, I could not share it with people on the Earth...

In hindsight, it is obvious that I should have been happy then. In the following hours I received amazing answers considering life, death and afterlife. However, at that very moment, I had no idea what awaited me. And I did not even think that during our conversations I would be the one who would tell them new things!

– 3 –

Yin was still outside the room, and I was left with my thoughts. I tried to get used to the new situation and to my new body. The truth was that it did not even occur to me to get up and look around, because I was still in shock. Later on, it turned out that I could not have gotten up even if I had wanted to, because my body was fastened to the chair. It would have been a great experience to walk in a child's body again, I was sure!

While I was waiting, I tried to sum up everything that I had heard so far. Of course, I already accepted that I was dead. And the fact that I was still alive in some kind of form was not so surprising at all. I had never believed that we would disappear after death, as if we had never existed.

I remembered my materialistic friends who had questioned the existence of the afterlife. I wished them to be there. I was so curious what they would say in this situation. I had often argued with those people, but we would always conclude that neither of the opinions could be confirmed with scientific facts and evidence. We understood that our discussions were in vain, because the result would always be a draw. However, I was proud that, apparently, I was the winner in the end…

But I could not accept my current situation that easy.

Yin said that I did not arrive at my final destination, to the afterlife, because they had stopped me somehow, and put my soul into another body. It was very disturbing for me that I could not finish my journey. I began worrying that this might affect my arrival to the afterlife. And because I was sure that Yin had not shared with me every detail of this experiment, I decided to ask some additional questions in order to feel more comfortable.

Yin still did not appear, so I kept thinking about the things that I had experienced so far. I found very interesting the communication they used. It made me wonder whether telepathy worked in every situation. For instance, if I thought about my hometown, what would Yin see who had never been there before? Would he see everything that I knew about that place, or just what I was thinking about it at that moment?

I was very curious about this, because Yin said that I would not possibly understand every thought of his, which I found a bit offensive but reasonable. For example, if I was talking about a nucleus or about quadratic equations to a four-year-old child, he could not understand a word either.

Probably, it disturbed me only because Yin assumed that I was not intelligent enough to understand him. However, my resentment did not last long and I gave him benefit of the doubt. At the very beginning, he could not know what kind of civilization I came from. They might have stopped the soul of a four-year-old or the soul of an adult coming from a not so advanced civilization. After all, it was not so long ago when we did not even know that the Earth was round and that there were other planets in the Universe.

Before Yin's arrival, I had just had enough time to think about one more thing. He said that, in his opinion, they were only a few thousand years ahead of us. I did not care why he had assumed that, but I wanted to know what one year meant to him. In my opinion, it is a very relative period of time, because a year consists of 365 days only on the Earth. If we were more distant from the Sun, the orbit of our planet would be longer, thus a year would also be longer. On Mars, for instance, a year consists of 700 Earth days. So, when he said a few thousand years, might he have meant much more or less?

"No," I heard my inner voice, but I could not see Yin anywhere. In the next moment he entered the room and he continued: "The universality of telepathy implies that in your mind a response will appear that is adjusted to *your* concept of time. That existing unit of time is a basic element from which a period of any length can be built up."

"This is logical," I said. "But in my defense, I began to use this kind of communication just a few minutes ago. It is still new for me..."

"It is normal that you have not become used to it yet."

"So, if there are only a few thousand years between us, does it mean that we will be the same as you are in a while?" I asked. "Will telepathy be used on the Earth by then?"

"You have mentioned that some of you already know how to use telepathy, haven't you?"

"Yes," I answered, "but it has not been proven, so it is not sure that if it really works."

"Well," began Yin, "in a civilization telepathy is formed slowly, step by step. Of course, this is not the case with you, because you arrived in a moment to this new, more developed body which is capable of such communication. So for you, this was a sudden change, but in a civilization, as I have mentioned already, this happens slowly, generation after generation. The time will come when you see the first signs without even realizing what is happening."

Then Yin turned to a machine, while I was thinking about an interesting phenomenon related to this. It had happened to me numerous times that, while walking on the street, I remembered a friend of mine all of a sudden. The thought of him came to me without any reason. And after a little while we met!

Of course, Yin heard these thoughts, so he responded immediately:

"Yes, these signs can be taken seriously. You recognized the brainwaves of another person and that is why you remembered him before the physical encounter. Our brain transmits identification signals, however, this cannot be considered as real communication. You made the first steps leading towards telepathy: you could recognize someone according to his brainwaves. Otherwise, everyone has different brain wavelengths..."

"...as everyone has different fingerprints and DNA!" I added.

"Exactly! So, this is not new for you. Great!"

I was glad that he praised me because, in the beginning, I had a feeling that Yin underestimated me. Anyway, I thought that I had learnt everything about telepathy, however, I had one more question:

"Don't you ever speak aloud?"

"No," answered Yin, and he turned to one of the machines again.

Then I remembered that previously I decided to ask him a few things related to the experiment. I waited for him to turn back and look at me. When this happened, I asked him:

"Can you explain me how this experiment will be carried out? How will you get me back here?"

"Are you interested in the scientific background?"

"Well... Yes."

"I will try to explain it simply, so that you can understand it."

"All right," I said.

"Think of all this as if you had a tracking system attached to your soul."

"How is that possible?"

"Your brainwaves will be perfectly synchronized with our machines. Can you understand it now?"

"Yes."

"And when you die," he continued, "when your mind leaves this body, we will still be able to detect its signs, because the soul is immortal. And in theory, we can bring you back here."

"Just in theory?"

"Well… We have not succeeded in it yet. We are sure that we are doing everything right, but whenever we try to bring a soul back, we always fail."

"And is it sure that when I leave this body, I will get to the same place where I would go if you had never stopped my soul?"

"Yes," he answered quickly.

"So, the fact that you stopped me in the middle of my journey, does not change anything, does it?"

"No, you can be sure in that," he said and we were quiet for a short time. Yin might feel that he did not convince me, so he continued: "If you take an object and drop it, what will happen?"

“It will fall down.”

“Yes. But if you stop it while it is falling, and then drop it again, it will continue falling in the same direction. This rule applies to everything that is made of matter. Objects fall only in one way just like the planets circulate only in one way...”

“The gravitation,” I thought.

“Exactly. And the soul also has its own path. When our consciousness leaves the body, it starts to follow it. These are universal laws. We have stopped your soul for a short period, but there is really no need to worry.”

“OK, I think I am beginning to calm down,” I said. “But why was it my soul that you stopped?”

“This happens randomly. We never know who will be stopped. Every soul, coming from whatever planet, will enter the afterlife through this passageway. We discovered it and sometimes we can catch a soul. Your consciousness is brought to this temporary brain by means of a special device, and you are fastened to the chair, because we do not want you to accidentally switch off the machine. Your soul cannot stay in this body without these machines. Our researches have shown that the soul can stay only in that body permanently, in which it was born.”

After hearing this explanation I became relaxed, and I was not afraid anymore that I might stay here. I understood that this was a temporary state and that there was only a little time left and I could be with my deceased loved ones again...

I became so relaxed that I began talking very honestly:

"You know, I really miss my loved ones. I was afraid that I would not see them again, but now I know for sure that this will happen soon."

"Well," began Yin, "we do not have an obvious proof that we will meet our deceased loved ones in the afterlife, because we have never succeeded in bringing back a soul. But all of our scientific researches suggest that this happens in the afterlife.

"So, the aim of this experiment is to get that obvious proof, right?"

"Yes. Once we had lots of questions just like you now, but we have found all the answers—except one. We still do not know what will happen with us after death. The longer we try to find the answer, the more curious we get."

"But it was you who told me before going out that you had theories."

"This is true, but we would prefer to have direct evidence. We found the passageway a long time ago, but we do not know where it leads exactly. Something very bad might also turn out about the afterlife…"

"For example?"

"For instance, that in the Universe every soul can get

a body only once. This would mean for us that it is not worth dying."

"Not worth dying?" I asked in my surprise. "You can decide whether you are going to die or not?"

"Yes. We can already do this. For example, I am a little over eight hundred years old."

"Eight hundred?"

"Yes."

"This is incredible!" I said. "But you are a child. And me too..."

"One day you will also find the mechanism in our organism which controls the process of aging. You will learn how to regulate your body to live a thousand years."

"Can we become immortal as well?"

"No, we cannot achieve that," answered Yin. "The living matter has its own limits. Our creators designed our bodies to live approximately eighty years. If we set our age with the proper genetic intervention, the final limit is a thousand years. But death is an unavoidable part of one's life. It is encoded in our DNA and we cannot erase it. Immortality can be achieved only in one way: if we put our soul in a new body that is the exact genetic copy the original. Our soul can stay permanently in a clone without machines. This is how we can gain another thousand years. The material existence begins with conception and ends with death. We can only make the period of time between the two last as long as possible. We can also delay aging. This is why we are able to live much of our long lives in a young body."

"This is unbelievable..." I said. Yin could see astonishment, and at the same time, thirst for knowledge on my face. I think he could see that I was absorbing his words.

"The Universe consists of matter and energy," he continued. "Both of them have a living and an inanimate version. For instance, oxygen, iron, carbon or water are inanimate materials, but the living beings are living materials. Gravitation, heat or electrical energy, or in other words the physical energy is inanimate, but the soul is living energy. Neither the matter nor the energy—let it be living or inanimate—disappear forever, they just change their forms. This is one of the main laws of the Universe. And human beings are very unique creatures, because we are the only living materials that contain living energy as well."

"So, does it mean that only humans have souls?" I asked.

"Yes."

"And what about animals?"

"They are only living materials," he answered. "There is no living energy in their bodies. And the same applies to plants. But we, human beings, are designed to be capable of accepting the soul."

I was listening to him carefully, I did not say a word, so Yin continued explaining:

"Of course, animals can communicate with each other, but these are only physical and chemical signs. The animals are not conscious. They do not realize the past or the future, they constantly live in the present. An animal is unable to plan ahead, because it cannot detect the time. For example, two animals cannot arrange a meeting the next day at an exact time...

"But the dogs bury bones and later on, if they need it, they know where to find them," I said.

"That is only memory and instinct. I think that you have also already found out that the biological instincts have only one aim: to keep the living being alive, thus to help the species preservation. In your example of dogs we can see clearly that they work exactly as they were designed," answered Yin and he stopped for a minute.

I have to admit, at that moment I could not believe that animals did not possess souls. I have always imagined that they have personalities, as we do, but they do not know how to speak, and of course, their intelligence is not as developed as ours. During my life I had a lot of cats and I always saw them as different personalities.

To this thought, Yin answered the following:

"If animals close their eyes, they only see darkness. And with their ears they can only hear those sounds that anyone else can in their presence. They cannot visualize pictures in their minds, they cannot use an inner voice."

Yin might see that he still did not really convince me, so he continued:

"Now you can see me and this room, right?"

"Yes."

"Close your eyes."

"I closed them."

"Imagine your house where you used to live."

"I did."

"Now imagine your cat. Can you see her?"

"Yes, I can."

"Imagine now her voice."

"I imagined."

"Well, you have just created a small world!"

I opened my eyes, but I could not really understand what Yin wanted to demonstrate with this.

"Haven't you ever asked how this is possible?" he asked me.

"Well, most probably we have been thinking about it without ever having come to an explanation."

"Animals cannot do such things at all, not mentioning

plants. Only we can do this, because our creators designed us in this way, and they left a part of themselves in us: the ability to create.

"So, we are living materials, like animals and plants, but we possess living energy as well," I summed up.

"That's right. The living materials are captured by their encoded instincts. Except humanity, every living being behaves as robots. They work in accordance with the previously fed codes. However, the living energy is endlessly free, because it is capable of creating anything! It seems that you are still in the transitional period. You are moving away from your animal instincts, and at the same time, you begin to resemble our creators more and more. The insatiable thirst for knowledge marks this period the best. By means of science you have probably also discovered that we were created by someone..."

Then Yin stopped talking, because Yang entered the room abruptly. He looked at Yin for a moment. I am sure he said something to him, however, I did not hear anything. Yin became excited which was very surprising, because since when we had met, he showed no emotions. He said only a few words to me:

"I have to go now, but I will try to come back as quickly as possible."

"Has anything gone wrong?" I asked.

"Far from it. We managed to catch another soul!"

– 4 –

The size of the building which I was staying in had not been my concern so far, but now I presumed that it must have been very big. It had at least one more similar room, where the other soul had just been stopped on its journey to the afterlife. I was much more interested in how the planet which I was staying on might look like. Was it similar to the Earth? And what were the people like? How many inhabitants were there? What did the plants and the animals look like?

In order to find the answers to my questions, I looked around carefully to see if I might find a window which would show me something from the outer world. Sadly, there were no windows in the room or—which I assumed to be more probable—all the windows were behind me.

The other five bodies were still motionless, sitting beside me. The previous conversation made me think that, although they were people, they were more like animals, because they did not have souls. They were still sitting with their eyes closed and with their heads turned down. It made me wonder how they would act if they had been awakened from this artificial dream—without getting a soul. Judging by what I had just heard about the difference between humans and animals, it was not so difficult to imagine the situation.

It was much more difficult to accept the fact that animals do not have souls. However, on second thought I could remember a number of arguments that confirmed Yin's statement. Finally, everything fell into place...

I remembered when the solar eclipse reached my city, the scientists had warned the people in advance that their pets would act as if it had been night. And that was exactly what happened: the insects, which could be found throughout the day, disappeared, the chirping of birds suddenly stopped—even though it was around noon.

Another similar example is that bears do not get fatter at the end of summer and during autumn, because they are aware of the coming winter. These are only instincts which are—as Yin said—encoded in them. It is obvious that animals do not feel the progress of time, and this means that they are not conscious either.

Regarding the plants, I had never assumed that they have souls. We learned at school that trees budded only once a year, in spring. But it had happened a few times that the autumn was not so cold, so the trees began to bud for the second time in the same year. Of course, the buds got frozen a few days later. It is obvious that we cannot talk about consciousness. This is only an encoded response to the change of the environment.

Yin also mentioned that we were in a transitional period in which we just began leaving our animal instincts. So—if I understood it well—we are partly still animals. And this explains many things. Primarily the wars, our tendency to destroy and our trait to solve the disagreements with violence. All these are undoubtedly animal instincts.

We know that the animals will do anything to protect their territory or to acquire a new one. Our wars are based on the same principles: we also fight for various goods. We organize our troops just like they are organized within many animal species: we fight in groups because the members are safer in numbers and can more easily defend themselves. However, by using our consciousness, we can produce weapons, thus we can kill more efficiently. In other words, this transitional period is not a brilliant era of ours, since we are both raging animals and brilliant minds at the same time. The scientific results are used to satisfy our still existing animal instincts.

Otherwise, we kill for the nourishment in the same way as the predators do. The difference is only that we think about the future, i.e. we plan. We are capable of raising domestic animals. We do this in order to kill them and eat them in the end. I cannot decide whether this is a positive or a negative characteristic of ours. But there is another difference which cannot be assumed to be positive at all: we, human beings, often kill for pleasure or because of hatred. And we all know that animals are not capable of doing such things.

For many people it is a pleasure and entertainment to do or watch a sport where our animal instincts are used. Boxing is a good example: it is nothing more than satisfying our animal instincts in a civilized way. Such fights contain rules and the participants—in most cases—follow them. However, sometimes they forget about the rules, because their animal instincts take over.

There is almost no field in our life for which I could not give a similar example. Just think about the mass panic attacks when people are trampled to death. Or when the infuriated sports fans howl, which resembles the behavior of an animal much more than human communication. Or when children ostracize their weakest peer exactly as animals do, or when they follow the most dominant one like the animals do with their leader of the pack.

As I kept thinking I had to realize that Yin was right. Anyway, why would I question someone's words who is a member of a much more advanced civilization?

I was still sitting alone in the room, when I remembered that Yin had said that the ability to create could be found only in us. I did not really understand what he meant. Was he only talking about that we could visualize anything by means of our thoughts?

I had to stop thinking, because Yang entered the room at that moment. I asked him immediately where his partner, I had been talking to, was.

"He is coming shortly," he answered.

I did not want to ask anything about that other soul, I had enough questions already. But before I could ask him my first one, Yang prevented me:

"Tell me about your planet!"

"Well, I do not know where to begin..." I said, thinking that the Earth and the human beings were so diverse that I could not explain it in a few sentences. And because I did not know whether Yang had heard anything about my conversation with Yin, I decided to sum up the facts that Yin said about us: "My civilization is only a few thousand years behind yours. We are living now in the era in which we are leaving our animal instincts and we begin to resemble our creators more and more. Our communication has not reached the level of yours yet, however, according to some signs it has begun developing."

"I understand," he said.

Probably he had some additional questions, but I was still impressed with the previous thoughts, so I asked him the next question quickly:

"How did you survive the transitional period?"

"Survive?" he asked me, and seemed to be surprised. "Everything was better back then! Of course, we could not live for so long as now and we had numbers of unanswered questions. But it is obvious that we had a much better life then..."

I was shocked when I heard this answer, because he

talked about the transitional period as a golden era. I was very confused, so I rephrased my question and asked it once again being more precise:

"How did you deal with the wars?"

Yang's face was devoid of expression, and he did not say a word. It was as if he became confused. I did not understand why he was silent, and I began feeling guilty as though I had said something wrong unwillingly. I just asked a question that interested me, but now I felt embarrassed that I might have offended him. I could only imagine that making wars was a so deep human instinct that even such an advanced civilization could not cope with it. I thought myself to be too naive when believing they had stopped killing each other.

"We do not need to talk about wars if you do not want to," I said.

But Yang kept being quiet, and I became more and more frustrated. Now I thought that he could not even understand what I was talking about. So, to make my conversation vivid, I began thinking about the wars of the twentieth century, because I knew he could see it as well.

After this, he said only a few words:

"We have never done similar things."

The answer confused me and I could not reply. Then Yang asked me:

"How many people live on your planet?"

"Around seven billion."

"Seven billion?" he asked me in disbelief.

"Yes. Is it many?"

"It is too many!"

Now it seemed that he was thinking carefully about something, but I could not hear anything. I suspected that he could control what he would transfer to me. Anyway, I continued the conversation:

"It is only these days that the Earth has become as populous. For example, fifty years ago there were only three billion of us. How many inhabitants does your planet have?"

"There are five million of us here."

"Just that few?"

"It is not few... There are too many of you! By doing this experiment we have met representatives of more than twenty civilizations and we have found out that every of those planets had only a few million inhabitants."

"Are there so many civilizations in the Universe?" I asked wonderingly.

"There are much more."

"How many?"

"I do not know the exact number, but according to the fact that the life seeds were spread in every direction, we think that human beings appeared on many planets."

"Who spread the life seeds?"

"Those who created them."

"You mean our creators?" I asked.

"Yes."

"So, isn't there only one creator?"

"Well, we believe that there are more of them, however, there might be only one."

"And how do you know that they spread the life seeds?" I asked skeptically. "This must have happened before the appearance of human beings."

"Haven't you found out?"

"Well... We have only theories about the beginning of life."

"So, haven't you discovered the life seeds?"

"No..."

"Well, I would like to tell you the story about the topic, but I came here to hear about *your* civilization. I am very interested in which way civilizations can develop. Fundamentally, every civilization is the same, but in the same way they are unique. And as I can see, your civilization is particularly unique... You know, this is our only joy in life. We have revealed almost every secret of our creators, so the only worthwhile event in our life is to make contact with members of another civilization."

I felt sorry for Yang, but it did not touch him. He continued:

"We were much happier when we did not want to know everything about the aim of our existence and about the working of the Universe. Curiosity destroyed everything! And as you have mentioned already, you are curious as well... You are on the wrong path."

"Why is it a problem if we are curious?"

"Because one day you will understand what the meaning of life is, and from that moment you will not enjoy it anymore."

"What do you mean?"

"Every question interests us until it is answered. Right? When we get the answer, the question is not interesting anymore. A question is a question, because we do not know the answer. Of course, now it is obvious that we should not have searched the meaning of life. But it is too late now…"

"I think I understand what you are talking about," I said. "Life is like a book. If you know what it is about, it is not for certain that you will really enjoy it..."

“Exactly!” said Yang. “Your approach to a familiar book is different from the approach to an unknown one.”

“So, you say that you have found out what the meaning of life is?”

“Yes.”

“And can you tell it to me?”

“Yes, but after that you will speak about your civilization. Deal?”

“Deal.”

– 5 –

I must say, I did not find this agreement to be very fair. To get the answer to the essential question what the meaning of life is, and in return just to talk about my own civilization that is not even as advanced as theirs... This did not seem correct at all. But I did not have twinges of conscience, because I could not give anything else, and anyway, I ended my life, so it did not really matter to me. And even the fact that my soul was temporarily in a living body did not change anything.

"Let's start with the information that there are two types of existence," said Yang.

"Matter and energy," I answered.

"Yes. Have you also discovered this?"

"Your companion had said this before he went out. Our body is living matter, our soul is living energy, and humans are the only creatures that exist in both forms."

"Exactly."

"However, I have to add that I do not really

understand the phrase living energy. It is the soul, isn't it?"

"Yes, it is."

"And what is our consciousness then?" I had to ask him this question, because we had talked about soul, living energy and consciousness so far.

"It is the same."

"And intelligence?"

"It is independent from the consciousness. Intelligence is an ability which is coded to other living beings as well, but it develops only in humans to such a great level."

"I see."

"So, in order to understand the meaning of life, first you have to know how life appeared. But before I explain it, I would like to ask how much you know about this? I am so curious! What do you think how life began?"

"Well… Our scientists claim that the living beings appeared accidentally from inanimate materials. This is the essence," I answered and I was not sure, but it seemed that Yang was shocked. I tried to save the situation, so I added quickly: "But actually we do not know anything about the beginning of life."

"Yes, I see that..."

"But how do you know it?" I asked. "You probably do not have any evidence."

"Of course we do! I can see that you have not had chance to examine ice from the comets so far."

"No, we have not," I answered.

"The life seeds are microorganisms designed by our creators. These cells travel on comets. They were sent into the Universe by an enormous explosion."

"Yes, I have heard about it. This is called the Big Bang."

"Sorry?" asked Yang.

"It is when nothing exploded and space, time, matter—in other words, everything—appeared."

"Do you believe that the matter came into existence from nothing?"

"Yes..."

"So, you think that the matter in the Universe appeared from nothing, and the life developed from this matter accidentally?" summed up Yang.

I have to admit, I felt like I was ashamed in the name of our scientists. I am supposedly a member of a more advanced civilization and I said such things... It seemed that Yang was disappointed with me, even though it was hard to guess anything from his face expression.

"At least, you know about the explosion..." he added.

"Yes..."

"But why do you believe that this explosion created space and time?"

"I do not know," I answered.

"The explosion, the signs of which you have had also found out, was the spreading of the life seeds. Space, time and matter have always existed."

"So, the Big Bang was only the spreading of the life seeds..." I repeated.

"The explosion was the best possible solution," continued Yang. "This is how the life seeds could get to every part of the Universe at incredible speed."

"But how do you know that this happened exactly in this way?"

"Well, we found out that our body was designed immediately after we began examining it. It was incredible and impressive at the same time when we discovered how complicated our bodies were. It is a real masterpiece! The more information we discovered about its functioning, the more confident we became about its intelligent design. But you do not have to worry! One day you will also understand that our bodies are similar to carefully designed machines consisting of millions of pieces that work in a perfect harmony. And not only our bodies are complicated but the cells that make them up as well...

"But we have also found it out!" I said a little resentfully.

"And you still think that all this developed accidentally?"

I felt embarrassed again, I could not say a word. Yang continued:

"We found the evidence on the comets in space. Have you found out that the comets are made up of ice?"

"Of course..." I said. "They have streaks because when they get near the Sun, the ice starts melting," I added as though I wanted to prove that the science on the Earth was not as bad as it might have seemed in the previous last few minutes.

"Exactly," agreed Yang. "Sooner or later the comets collide with a planet, and after that the ice becomes water. Where the conditions are good, the life seeds begin developing. First, very simple beings appear. According to the plan, their aim is to create conditions good enough for more complex living beings to develop. And when these unicellular organisms detect favorable conditions, from their small group multi-cellular beings appear suddenly. The other, larger part of the unicellular organisms does not develop, because they have to satisfy the multi-cellular beings' need for nourishment and living. This is how more and more complex forms of life appear, however, at the same time those organisms from which the more complex beings were developed also remain. This happens on every planet. First, animals appear in the water, then they reach the mainland and the outcome of the gradual development will be human beings. The main goal of the evolution is the appearance of humans, the only creatures that are able to accept a soul. The life seeds, which were spread by our creators, reach the peak when human beings appear."

"And you say that you have proofs for this?"

"Yes, we do. The simple microorganisms that we found in the ice of comets contain the genetic codes of all animals and plants, and also the blueprint of the human body as the final goal! And we have practical proofs as well, since in a few months we succeeded in raising a human being from the cell originating from the ice of a comet."

"This is simply unbelievable!" I said. "If one day we also succeeded in this, it would change everything on the Earth..."

"Then you will finally understand that life did not happen accidentally…"

"Yes..."

"Most of the planets," continued Yang, "do not have proper conditions. However, where each component can be found, the process of creating human beings can begin. This happens relatively fast. Considering how long it takes for the first living organisms to create the appropriate conditions for humankind, turning into humans takes just a minute.

"According to this, human beings can be found on every planet?" I asked.

"No. Only on planets that the life seeds reached, and where the conditions are just right."

"Yes, I understand this, but I have some questions."

"I thought so," said Yang. "I understand you entirely. Curiosity and the desire for knowledge are still enormous in you... What do you want to know?"

"I do not know where to begin... If I understood you well, the main goal of the evolution is the appearance of human beings. Right?"

"Yes."

"Then I do not understand the dinosaurs… We have found out that there was a very long period of time when the reptiles ruled our planet. They inhabited the mainland, the seas and the air in the most various ways."

"This is really interesting..." said Yang. "We have not heard of such things so far, but knowing the rules of the evolution, this is not strange at all."

"What do you mean?" I asked. "Doesn't it look like that the main goal of the evolution were reptilians? Because if that asteroid impact had not happened, human beings might never have appeared on the Earth..."

"There are lots of places where the life seeds reached and the development began, but human beings never appeared. It is nothing strange. The evolution follows a precise timetable, but there are plenty of reasons why it cannot reach its aim. As I have mentioned, in the ice of the comets the blueprint of humans can be found as the final goal, but anything can stop this process. After our creators spread the life seeds, they cannot control the asteroid impacts, the unbearable climate changes or other catastrophes..."

"OK, I understand this," I said.

"And the reason why the reptiles inhabited your whole planet is that life was created to be extremely flexible."

"The adaptation..." I thought.

"Yes. So, you have already found that out. Our creators made us adapt to various conditions in order not to become extinct during a small environmental change. It is incredible how much attention they paid to details. If life was not so flexible, there would be no human beings on the planets. Thus, everything would be senseless..."

"So, this is the meaning of life?"

"Of course not! This is only the meaning of the evolution," answered Yang. "Human beings are the ultimate aim of the evolution, because we are the most important works of our creators. The microorganisms, the plants and the animals exist only to ensure nourishment and bearable living conditions for us. They exist in order to make every living aspect as good and flexible as possible, before the appearance of human beings."

"I understand," I said after some thinking. "Everything is clear, and if I think about it, it is nothing new. We have also recognized these connections, but we do not have any evidence that *we* are the purpose of the creation. What is more, the fact of creation, or intelligent design, is not accepted by everyone. We can trace back life to the first cells, but we do not know how they came to be."

"We have never met such a civilization," said Yang. "You have found out so many things, and you still think that life happened accidentally..."

It had been unpleasant so far, I even regretted telling him our scientific views about the origin of life, and sincerely, I was tired of the fact that he was constantly mentioning it, so this time I continued the conversation without feeling embarrassed:

"Our evolution-theory has a point that is the total opposite of what you have said. The scientists on the Earth think that the change of form of life happens very slowly, but you have said that the more complex living beings always appeared suddenly. You have also said that you succeeded in developing a human being from the simplest microorganisms just in a few months. Doesn't it take millions and millions of years?"

"We have seen with our own eyes that the change in species happens suddenly, but the whole procedure—the creation of man from the first cell—is very slow indeed," said Yang.

"But only a few months?"

"Of course, it can last millions of years on a lifeless planet. We put the life seeds in an artificially created environment that accelerated the natural processes. But essentially, it is the same. As soon as an acceptable environment evolves, more developed living beings appear. And the last stage is always a human being."

"So, according to this, in the past an aquatic animal suddenly changed into a land one?"

"No. There are no such examples that an aquatic animal gives birth to a terrestrial one. There is a transitional species between them. Maybe this species is extinct on your planet, and in this case I understand why you cannot imagine how life emerged from the water. This type of species was designed in order to be able to live on the land and in the water as well..."

"The amphibians..." I thought.

"So, they are not extinct…" said Yang. "Anyway, when the environment is favorable, the first terrestrial animals appear all of a sudden."

"But how can an animal know whether the conditions are good enough?"

"How do you know that you need to breath, or when you need to blink in order to avoid your eyes get dry?"

I did not say a word, I was listening carefully.

"The first amphibian," continued Yang, "appeared from an egg of a sea creature. Later on, a number of its descendants, the so-called tadpoles, did not become frogs but they became the first reptiles. Even though they were not living entirely on the mainland, they did not reproduce in water as amphibians did but on the mainland. Their descendants produced the first real terrestrial animals. After this, a few steps were left until the appearance of human beings. And depending on how much time is needed for the new evolutionary step, certain species can reproduce in various types due to the adaptation. Dinosaurs inhabited your whole planet because, for some reason, the next evolutionary step could not happen on time. They had to wait, so they had much time to populate the planet."

"I think I get it..."

"Suppose there is a planet where there is no land, only water. Evolution would stay in an aquatic form of life for long, and an incredibly wide variety of aquatic animals and plants would appear there. One of the reasons of the high flexibility of living beings is that, if necessary, the evolution can wait. There might be long detours, but when the appropriate conditions are met, the final destination would be near!"

"This is very logical," I said.

"Evolution includes all the necessary preparations for the appearance of the human beings. If people appeared directly from the life seeds, they would die immediately due to the lack of plants that produce oxygen. What is more, this could not even occur, because human bodies are made up of previously existing simple organisms: cells."

"Yes, now I get it. I am not sure of one thing only. The first modern humans appeared suddenly from the cavemen?"

"Exactly," answered Yang. "When the development of the brain reached a certain level, the last generation of caveman mothers did not give birth to cavemen but to modern people. This was a sudden change, and due to the difference in the intellectual levels, the result was that parents did not understand their children who had souls, or in other words, consciousness."

"Yes, it is now quite clear," I said, and thought that something similar is happening nowadays as well. Parents hardly understand their children who are using the modern technological achievements so easily. There is a huge gap between them, so in this sense children are much more developed than their parents, although this difference is obviously not at all as big as it was between the caveman and the modern man.

Yang nodded like he was approving my thoughts, but I remembered a contradiction:

"Your companion has said that telepathy develops slowly, from generation to generation. Isn't it also supposed to appear directly, with a sudden jump?"

"No," said Yang. "Don't forget that we, human beings, are not only living materials. The sudden jumps are the characteristics of the living organisms. But what you have asked now, concerns the development of the soul and not the development of the body."

"Does our soul develop as well?" I asked in surprise.

"Yes! Slowly and gradually. To be able to prove this was the greatest scientific success of our civilization! The discovery of the materialized soul explained everything that we had not understood until then. We could not believe at first, but it turned out that our soul was evolving, even though it should not be the case."

"Why?"

"We believe that an unexpected error occurred, and as a result we began to resemble our creators too much. Slowly but surely, from generation to generation, we are going to become as they are. That is why a tremendous curiosity developed in us, which also did not appear suddenly but came gradually. It is slowly growing and developing. The more we learn, the greater is our desire for knowledge. We waste our time trying to reveal our creators' secrets, and in this way, we are getting as far as possible from the initial purpose of our existence," finished Yang. Then he paused and turned to one of the machines. It seemed as if he was not speaking in order to give me time to think about what I had heard. Whether this was the case or not, there was no doubt that I received some information that could not have been easily understood…

And then it dawned on me! As long as I had lived, or

to be more accurate: as long as I had lived on the Earth in my own body, the proponents and opponents of the theory of evolution agreed only on one thing: evolution does not provide a perfect explanation of the origin of life. It only explains how species had formed from each other and how a creature can have so many variants. Thus, Darwin discovered only the order of appearance of species as well as that particular flexibility, in other words, the adaptation.

His biggest fault was that he tried to imagine the origin of life based on these discoveries. Now, that I had learnt about the life seeds and their role, I do not understand those who say that evolution proves that life appeared accidentally. Darwin just recognized that the process of becoming a human could be traced back to the simplest organisms. But why would this exclude the intelligent design, i.e. the creation?

It is also interesting to note that Darwin imagined the appearance of the more developed species as incredibly slow transitions and not as sudden changes—despite many fossils available even in his time. The theory of the slow transformation has not ever been proved. According to the fossils the new species always appeared "completely formed", so when they appeared they were extremely complex, in other words, perfect.

The more I think about it, the less I understand this clinging to millions of years long gradual transformation theory. After all, there are so many creatures on the Earth being transformed into a very different kind of living being in front of our eyes! The above-mentioned tadpole, not only in evolutionary terms but measured in human time, becomes partially a land animal in a minute! And a caterpillar also does not need millions of years to change into a flying butterfly... Examples for sudden jumps could be found every day in nature!

And as the new information fell into place, I began to realize more and more things. Our scientists do not really know to explain how it is possible that, according to the archaeological records, at one moment the man resembled a cave animal and in the next minute he turned into a highly intelligent creature who could make beautiful paintings, lifelike statues, established cities, dealt with animal husbandry, cultivated the land, could speak, read, write and count. Well, relying on the knowledge that I had gained a few minutes ago, I can already explain this: the answer is that modern people who had souls also appeared as sudden as any other living creature before them!

However, it was still strange that the modern man could not imagine how ancient civilizations were capable of such an incredible architectural accomplishment such as the pyramids. I learned from Yang that the science was gradually developing, but it was not logical that the first civilizations on the Earth were apparently more advanced than the next ones...

And it was also not clear to me that after the completion of the physical evolution, why did the soul begin its gradual development? Why did Yang think that this was not how it should have happened? What kind of unexpected error was he talking about? And what is the materialized soul which became the greatest scientific discovery of his civilization?

In any case, another mosaic fell into place. Yin had said before he left the room that we were different from the animals, because we had the ability to create. Then I did not quite understand what he was talking about. I thought that he was referring only to the creative power of our thoughts, but I finally understood. Urban planning and building cities, animal and crop production, and the best example: the art is being more than the creation itself! Of course this is what distinguishes us from the animals!

Yang certainly heard my thoughts, because when he looked at me again, for a moment, it seemed as if he was smiling. It was a sort of look that resembled a radiant smile of satisfaction appearing on our faces when we make somebody understand something. This is how teachers smile when they see that their students understand and absorb the subject.

"I think now it is time for you to speak," said Yang.

"But you have not told me what the meaning of life is!"

"You do not understand it even now?"

"I think it is better if you say it, rather than I begin guessing."

But before this could happen, Yin walked in. He told something Yang that I could not hear again. Yang said only the following:

"I have to go now."

"But you will come back, won't you? We have not finished this conversation!" I said a little irritably.

"Don't worry, I will be back. But I think you have already got the point!" he said.

Then Yang left the room, and Yin gave me a glass of that clear liquid once again.

– 6 –

Yin was dealing with one of the machines—he was probably preparing for the experiment—while I was still under the impression of the previous conversation. I finally understood the evolution! However, it seemed to be a very selfish idea at first that every microorganism, plant and animal exists only to keep human beings alive.

Of course, I know it very well that if certain microorganisms, plants or animals did not exist, we would not live either. Imagine an everyday lunch: the meat of an animal, for instance chicken, is being consumed with some vegetable, for instance, potato, and later, everything is being decomposed by the bacteria in our colons. This example really illustrates that some organisms exist only to keep us alive.

However, there are many living beings which, apparently, have nothing to do with people's life. For example, lions: they do not produce oxygen and we do not eat their meat. From our point of view they are entirely unnecessary, and what is more, we are even threatened by them. But still, this species exists independently of us and at the same time with us. This contradiction annoyed me a bit, so I decided to ask Yin or Yang about it at a suitable time.

But at that moment I had more important questions. For instance, I could hardly wait for Yang to finally tell me what is the meaning of life. I thought it would not be fair if I discussed it with Yin. After all, only the answer was missing in order to finish that topic.

I could have asked him about the other soul which caused him to leave the room. Or I could have informed him that I understood what kind of creation he mentioned, when he was talking about the difference between humans and animals. I could have also asked why their civilization had never waged wars. There were so many things to ask, but when Yin turned from the machine and when he looked at me, I could say only the following:

"Is this water?"

After a longer break I used my speech organs again. It was still frightening to hear that child voice.

"It consists mostly of water, but there are proteins, carbohydrates, minerals and vitamins in it as well. Everything that is necessary to keep our bodies alive," he answered.

"Don't you ever eat?" I asked the question by means of telepathy again, and I realized that I was not hungry at all since I had been in my new body.

"Unfortunately, we had to give up solid food. It is

true that we can live even a thousand years, but this is possible only if we take care of our body. Solid food would ruin our circulatory system in 100-120 years. So, if we want to live a thousand years, we must consume this liquid only. But we cannot complain, it is we who wanted such long lives..."

"I see," I said.

"Yes, our bodies are young, but the food that we eat is an external factor. Our circulatory system is adversely affected by continual passing of processed solid food through it. But for instance, in case the air is clear, our lungs can bear the gas exchange without any problem even for a thousand years. Also the kidney, the liver and the brain work flawlessly."

"According to this, you will die as children, won't you?"

"No," answered Yin. "Originally, the human body is designed to get stronger gradually, then it begins to deteriorate gradually and finally it stops working. We rescheduled this in a way that instead of eighty years we can live the maximum, approximately a thousand years, by spending most of the time in a young and a strong body. According to the original schedule, we reach our teenage years as you do, but after that we have a nine-hundred-year break. But in the end, of course, we will also become old and we will die. This is the way of life, everyone has to undergo it, that is how we are designed."

"Yes, when we first talked, you mentioned that death

could not be deleted from our genes."

"This is true," he confirmed.

"But according to what you have said, it seems that we are designed to die around eighty, but there are lots of people who pass away much earlier..."

"You are right. But the accidents, in which some people die at a very young age, cannot be foreseen."

"I do not mean that now but rather the deadly diseases."

"Sorry?"

"For example, the epidemics that killed millions of people long ago. Plague, cholera, typhoid, Ebola, malaria and the HIV-virus, for which there is still no cure, or the influenza that can cause fatal complications and other viruses, bacteria..."

"What are these?" asked Yin.

"These are diseases that kill."

"I have never heard about such things!" said Yin and the signs of shock could be seen on his face.

Now, it was time for me to be shocked! Is it possible that they do not have and they have never had any diseases? I could not believe it!

"No one has reported such things from other planets either," added Yin.

"Are we the only one who has diseases then?"

"Apparently, yes."

"But why?"

"There must be a reason."

"And how is it possible that you did not have wars either?!" I asked heatedly.

"Wars?"

"Yes!"

Since I had talked about wars only with Yang, I began recalling some of the most terrible scenarios of the Second World War, including the atomic bomb, in order to make Yin understand what I was talking about.

"Is this what happens on your planet?" he asked.

"Yes!"

"But why do you use your scientific achievements to destroy people?"

"Because we are still in the transitional period!" I answered. "Our animal instincts are still strong, thus we use science in this way as well. How is it possible that you have never had wars?"

"Why would we have wars?" he asked. "Why would we kill each other?"

I was very embarrassed, obviously because I had to

admit that we took wars for granted. The truth is that we cannot even imagine life without them, because they existed from the beginning of our civilization. As science evolved, the wars evolved with it. It is no exaggeration to say that we consider that peace is only a temporary state between two wars.

"Something went terribly wrong on your planet," Yin said.

"What do you mean?"

He was just about to reply when Yang entered the room. They looked at each other, and then Yin told me that he would be back soon. He left the room, but Yang stayed with me.

"So, where did we stop?" he asked. "Have you found out what the meaning of life is?"

"I am not thinking about it at all!" I answered nervously.

"What were you discussing after I had left?"

"We were talking about the fact that you had not had wars, diseases and moreover, they did not happen on any other planet in the Universe, just on the Earth!"

Since Yang, just like his partner, was ignorant of the topic, I familiarized him with the notion of fatal diseases. After that, he said only this:

"Life was not designed for such horrible things."

Then I remembered our conversation that we had had before he left the room. The part when I found out that they had never had wars. At first, he did not even understand what I was talking about, but when he understood it, he immediately asked how many people lived on my planet. When I answered, he began thinking about something carefully, however, I did not hear a word.

Obviously, he did not ask the question without a reason, so I felt justified to refer back to it:

"What were you thinking about when you found out that there were seven billions of people on my planet? Why did you ask it at all?"

"I remembered our theory about the death of civilizations. We believe that the members of a more advanced civilization can cause their own extinction in two ways. The first one is killing themselves accidentally by using science, the other one is over-reproduction leading to lack in food and water."

"And we are threatened by both at the same time..." I concluded bitterly.

The previous depressing moments made me forget the amazing realizations for a while.

Is the Earth really such a bad place? Why does it happen that both of their theories regarding the death of civilizations are present on the Earth? And to make things even worse, unlike Yang's peaceful assuming, we would not accidentally cause our destruction by using scientific results...

Obviously, they thought that during the development of science some civilizations might find out what nuclear energy was and might use it—for peaceful purposes, of course—but unintentionally, let's say as a result of an accident, a chain-reaction might begin which could cause the planet's flora and fauna to die out. I do not even dare to think about how shocked Yang was, when he found out that the atomic bomb had been thrown on innocent people intentionally…

It might be also possible that they imagined extinction by science in an entirely different way. They might only think about the environmental pollution caused by the technological progress which is fatal because, sooner or later, the water and the air would not be clear enough to keep us alive.

However, in my opinion, Yang thought about something else when he asked how many people lived on the Earth. And why did he go silent when he received the answer? What was he thinking about? Maybe that we had over-reproduced and we were fighting for nourishment and water of which there were less and less? Well, this is a logical thought if we keep in mind that losing our animal instincts did not happened yet. The struggle for food and water are obviously animal instincts, but the capability of producing weapons of mass destruction is a human trait. However, on our planet there had been wars even when the science was at its beginning, and it is not true that we are fighting only because of lack of water and food...

Regardless how Yin and Yang imagined the extinction of the civilizations, we had been aware of this fact for a long time. It is almost a cliché that a nuclear war can destroy the planet's flora and fauna and it is also clear that we cannot reproduce indefinitely. Therefore, these were not new realizations at all.

It was a much bigger surprise that fatal diseases existed only on our planet. Why? And is there any connection between pathogens, wars and the fact that seven billion people live on our planet? It looks like that these are specific to the Earth only.

Most probably Yang was thinking about the same

thing, because the next conversation resembled an interrogation. Yang behaved like a detective, however, I answered everything, because I knew he would share his conclusion with me in the end.

"Are there as many other living beings as people on your planet?" he began.

"There are lots of plants and animals," I answered. "There are so many that our scientists cannot even count them. We can only guess their number."

"Are there so many of them?"

"Yes. There are millions of different plant and animal species on the Earth. Not to mention the number of the extinct species that, according to the fossils, existed before us."

Then it seemed that Yang remembered something, but he did not want me to hear it. I was sure that he began understanding it...

"Do you have any idea when the life seeds reached your planet?" he asked.

"I think the oldest traces of life are nearly four billion years old," I replied.

"And were there other periods when one species populated your whole planet like the dinosaurs did?"

"Well, I do not know much about it, but according to our scientists, before and after the dinosaurs there were several plant and animal species which disappeared as the ancient reptiles did."

"And have you found out what caused these extinctions?"

"Asteroids, series of volcano eruptions, global warming, ice age, and something similar."

"How many mass extinctions were there?"

"Five. During these almost every species got extinct," I answered.

Then Yang stopped talking and began thinking about something. However, I was so curious that I had to ask him directly:

"Do you have an idea what went wrong on my planet?"

"I think I do. But first, I will tell you how it happened on our planet. You will understand the differences more easily if you are familiar with the original plan."

"All right," I said.

"We have three thousand plant and animal species."

"Only that few?"

"It is not few. You can see that human beings appeared here as well, what proves that three thousand species are quite sufficient for the evolution's goal. In fact, it is you that have incredibly many species on your planet! The life seeds reached our planet ten million years ago, but on your planet it happened four billion years ago. Life began developing here much later, but still, we exist at the same time with you, and our civilization is even more advanced."

"But how is this possible?"

"You have already given the answer!"

"Really?" I asked in surprise.

"Yes. The evolution on your planet has often been interrupted for various reasons, but it has always restarted. Life has evolved in its regular way but—before human beings could appear—something always happened that erased the most complex beings causing a change in evolution: it had to begin developing again from the first step, from the most elementary forms of life. And as we know, these living beings can endure the most extreme conditions. They are designed this way which is not surprising, because they have to survive the very long journey in the ice of comets and the impacts as well. You have surely found microorganisms which cannot be destroyed either by heat or freeze."

"Yes, we have."

"Therefore, the most primitive organisms," Yang continued, "are very tough, because they form the base to every animal and plant. People, on the other hand, have entirely different roles. Our aim is neither only the survival nor the creation of the necessary conditions for other organisms. It is a general rule that the more developed a living being is, the more fragile it is. It can more easily die out. Due to the big catastrophes that you have mentioned, the majority of the terrestrial beings became extinct on your planet. In such cases, there is always an enormous pause in the evolution, because the primary organisms need millions of years to make the conditions as they were before the catastrophe. Even such a big catastrophe could be imagined that made the planet a worse place than it was before the life seeds had reached it. And because the life seeds arrived to your planet four billion years ago, it is obvious why there are fatal diseases."

"Why?" I asked.

"The series of the catastrophes did not hurt the tough microorganisms. Having adapted for four billion years continuously, they had plenty of time to strengthen! Those microorganisms have an enormous advantage regarding the later creatures, especially the human beings—the most sensitive ones. We do not have such pathogens on our planet, because nothing interrupted our evolution. The primitive life forms did not have the opportunity to strengthen here."

"Yes, I understand it now," I said. "We fight against various pathogens, but apparently, they have such a big advantage that we will never defeat them..."

And then I remembered that we had developed the vaccination against flue almost in vain, because the virus mutates every year and it creates new strains. Of course, there are illnesses which we could defeat: these are not fatal anymore, but earlier in the past, the same epidemics could cause the death of one-third of a continent's population.

"This is another thing our creators did not count on. Another designing mistake..." Yang interrupted me. "They did not think that the flexibility, which they gave to microorganisms in order not to die out easily due to environmental changes, could even lead to the destruction of their main creature, the human being."

"This is unbelievable," I said.

"But there is something that the evolution's constant restarting does not explain."

"What is it?"

"There are plenty of you," answered Yang. "And not only of you, human beings but as you have already mentioned, there are millions of plant and animal species as well. On your planet something affects life favorably, because even after a series of catastrophes the planet gets fully populated again. You said that the ancient reptiles inhabited the mainland, the water and the air as well. What is it that can cause millions of variations at every evolutionary step on your planet?"

"I do not know," I said. "But it is true that there is life wherever we go on the Earth."

"Does your planet have any specific characteristics? Is there a disproportionately huge amount of some kind of material, maybe?"

“Water!” I remembered immediately. “The planet’s three quarters consist of water.”

“Of course!” said Yang. “This explains everything!”

“Really?” I asked in surprise.

“There are so many species due to the enormous quantity of water! Seven billion people are not that many at all if there is so much water and nourishment. Only one-tenth of our planet consists of water, and this is why here cannot be more than a few thousands of plant and animal species and more than a few millions of people. And the amount of water on your planet also explains why you make wars!”

“It explains the wars, too?” I was confused.

“Yes! You know that the water originates from comets, don’t you?”

“Yes, we know.”

“Well, according to how much water you have, we can assume that, measuring in cosmic scale, you are very close to the place from which the comets were sent by the Big Bang. I do not exclude the possibility that your planet is the nearest one to this place! Due to this, there were many impacts which caused a disproportionate amount of water. And the comets did not bring only ice...”

“...but a lot of life seeds as well,” I ended Yang’s sentence.

"That is right. Most probably, the large amount of life seeds began developing in many separate ways. This can be the only explanation!"

"But I still do not understand."

"I think that on your planet more independent evolutionary processes had begun and many of them finished!"

"More evolutions?"

"Yes," Yang answered. "Most likely, life emerged from water to mainland on many places, but obviously, it did not happen at the same time. Therefore, it is not surprising at all that you have such a variety of living beings."

"But how are our wars related to this?" I asked.

"Don't you understand? On your planet the conditions for life are so good that more evolutionary processes were completed. More human species evolved! If my theory is correct, then the seven billion of people on your planet are not as similar to each other as we are here."

"This is true. We are not so similar..." I said. "We are very different."

"Then I am right. This is the explanation!"

"But genetics has shown that the people who live nowadays on our planet have one and the same ancestor. According to the archeological findings, there really were different human species in the distant past, but they all got extinct except the species we all originate from."

"This is quite interesting..." said Yang and he became quiet for a second. "I thought that on your planet still lived many different human species and this caused the animosity. But according to what you have just said, human species blended in the past. And an ancient blending of species is just a much better scientific explanation for your wars!"

"Ancient blending?" I asked.

"Yes. On your planet the more evolutions did not have any serious consequences until the appearance of human beings. Maybe just the unbelievable variety of plant and animal species. But when people began appearing on different parts of the planet, animosity appeared as well. According to our creators' original plan, on one planet there should be only one evolution, and in the end a single human species should evolve. But on your planet more human species appeared, and each of them could think that the goal of the evolution was their own species. They had every right to think this is true. In the animal kingdom we can see animosity only if several rivals are competing for the same role. And this leads to the conclusion that you are still fighting, because it became an instinct due to the ancient blending."

"This may be true," I said. "Many times we cannot even explain what our problem is with the one who we hate. This is really almost a basic instinct. The reason is very often just that the one who we detest is different in something. We do not like him, because he is not similar to us. What is more, we think that he is inferior. The people on the Earth always feel the need to divide the humanity into groups, which can be done on whatever basis. And as you have said, certain groups of people feel that *they* are the one on the peak of evolution, not somebody else. They believe that *their* group is better and more valuable than others. This might be the basis of the superior race theories, religious fanaticism and other kinds of general division among people. And now, I have found out the reason for it."

Then I remembered how it happens in practice...

"This is terrible!" Yang said. "According to the original plan, hatred towards others is not coded into humans! But you are able to hate and destroy others only because you think that they are not like you. For example, just because the color of their skin or the way they think is different."

"Sadly, this is true. But not everyone acts in this way," I said. "Otherwise, you are not entirely the same either. For instance, the color of your face is white but the color of your partner's face is a bit darker."

"Yes, but this does not mean that our planet also has or had more human species. This is only the result of the adaptation which occurs among the same species. The people who live or come from a sunnier part of the planet always have a darker skin."

"This is true," I said.

"And are there people who are similar to us in appearance?"

"Yes, of course," I answered. "If you came to the Earth, no one would think that you originate from another planet."

Yang was not surprised at all.

"So, according to the original plan, everyone should look like you?" I asked.

"No," he answered. "Our creators could not know on which part of the planet the first human beings would appear. This is why the pigment in our skin is capable of a quick adaptation. We showed up on the less sunny part of the planet, and that is the reason why our skin is lighter. However, among our ancestors there were groups who migrated to south, thus their descendants have a darker skin. But we are all products of the same evolution, and that is why our descendants will always have the same basic characteristics. No noticeable physical and mental differences can appear among us."

"But I still do not understand why there are so big differences on the Earth," I added.

"Because of the ancient blending," Yang said. "Your species is the result of combining more human species. Thus, it is true that you are members of one human species, but it is a blended species. As we have already said, the reason for your wars could be found in this. On our planet we do not treat each other as enemies, because we have no reason to think that the other one is different. But your characteristic of not tolerating people who are different from you, can be traced back to your ancient ancestors. And due to the fact that you are the descendants of an ancestor resulting from more species being combined, being blended has become your basic characteristic. This, like other attributes, is inherited from generation to generation according to the rules of genetics. And if my theory is correct, then on your planet the physical and mental differences among the children of the same parents and even between the parents and their children are enormous."

"Yes, you are right," I agreed. "But there are similarities as well."

"We have similarities only."

"Unbelievable..."

"The blending, which is a decisive factor in your genes, manifests in a way that the new born child inherits a random amount of the ancient species' characteristics. At the time, human species that blended were at different stages of development, so if someone inherits more genes from a more advanced ancient species, he will be more intelligent. On our planet the same genes are passed from generation to generation, but on the Earth an infinite number of variations can occur."

"Yes," I said. "The fact that on our planet any intellectual level can appear at any race proves that we are all descendants of the same species."

"So, you are very varied, aren't you?"

"Yes, we are. However, we have ethnic groups whose members are much similar. I mean, in their physical appearance."

"This can also be explained by adaptation. After some time, groups were formed from the ancient blended species, and they migrated to different places where they adapted to the local conditions. The color of their skin changed according to the weather, their body type changed according to the nourishment they could find in that area. And because they reproduced among each other, after some time, they almost became equal in their appearance. This is also why we are so alike."

Then Yang stopped talking for a while, and the pieces fell into their place once again. I realized that I had totally misunderstood the so-called transitional period! Until now, I believed that hatred, wars and the fact that some people behave like animals, were normal for this period. How could I assume that our creators would willingly code hatred into us?

"Now I can understand you entirely," Yang said.

"What do you mean?"

"I see why you could still not find out what the meaning of life is. You possess all the scientific discoveries that are needed to answer this question, but diseases, hatred and wars just do not fit into the picture!

You could not know that these terrible things were not part of the original plan. And these mistakes—which could not be foreseen by our creators—only confused you..."

"So, I think it is high time you told me what the meaning of life is."

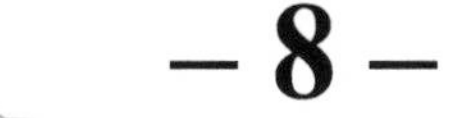

– 8 –

"I would like to emphasize," Yang began, "that our explanation of the meaning of life is based on pure guessing. It is simply impossible to find direct evidence in this topic. Where could we find data showing our creators' intentions while designing us?"

"Probably nowhere," I answered.

"Only when we pass away our theory can be proved. Most probably, we will get only in the afterlife the answer whether we were right or not. One of the aims of our experiment is the avoidance of death in order to get to know the truth. We hope that we will be able to bring you back from the afterlife and then you can tell us everything..."

"Yes, I know," I said impatiently.

"So, we believe that we have sufficient facts in order to state: we know the answer. And no one questions it."

"I will not either, just say it!" I urged him.

"When we found the life seeds in the ice of the comets and read the genetic plan showing that human beings were the final goal, we made a logical conclusion that the one who had created us surely had some kind of intention. Every scientific research shows one potential possibility…"

"And what is it?" I asked impatiently.

"Let's see why we, people, differ from the animals. What are the things that are only our characteristics?"

"We have souls, so we are conscious and we can also create," I summed up the things Yin has told me recently.

"Yes. These characteristics make us human. The most primitive organisms are very tough, because they are the base to every living being…"

"Yes, we have already discussed it," I said while becoming more and more impatient.

"…but humans are the exact opposite of them," Yang finished his sentence. "In case of a catastrophe we will be the first to die, because we are not so tough. We have been given an entirely different role. We are at the peak, thus we have only one thing to do: to enjoy the beauty of the world."

Yang stopped talking. I realized only after three or four seconds that I received the answer I had been waiting for so long.

"Sorry?" I asked.

"The meaning of life is to enjoy the material existence. This is something that no other living beings can do but people!"

Yang might have noticed that I could not easily accept his answer, so he began explaining:

"Do you know what the difference is between the skin of a man and an animal? It is enough to think of our nearest kin in the animal kingdom."

"Well… I think there is no such big difference," I answered. "The first thing that came to my mind is that we have less hair."

"This is the difference that can be seen from outside," Yang said. "But it is good for a start. You have surely found out that the human skin, unlike animal skin, is the only one that is not capable of protection from environmental influences."

"Now, that you have mentioned it… Yes, it is really true."

"This happens because our skin, just as our whole body, was designed for something else. The animal skin has a role to provide protection from large temperature fluctuations and in general, from environmental changes. Their skin is much more resistant than ours. However, this is not surprising, because the human skin does not have to protect us from the outer world. On the contrary—our skin is extremely sensitive due to a lot of nerve endings, so we are not only capable of detecting small temperature changes and physical stimuli, but we can also determine the material of an object just by touching it. Due to this sensitivity, our skin cannot protect us from the environmental influences. Otherwise, it is impossible to design a skin capable of both protection and detection of pleasant stimuli at the same time."

"This is interesting indeed," I said. "But can we conclude only from this that we were designed to enjoy the beauty of the material existence?"

"Every sign shows that," Yang replied. "Here is another example. No other living being can enjoy eating. Most of the animals do not even feel tastes. Mostly by smelling the food they decide whether to eat it or not. This is coded into them. They eat, and what is more, they do everything based on their instincts. Food consumption is only an instinct in the animal kingdom, but human beings are capable of sorting and mixing flavors in order to enjoy the prepared dishes as much as possible."

"This is getting more and more interesting..." I added.

"And then there is reproduction" Yang continued. "For every animal, plant and microorganism this is only an instinct, but it is something more for human beings! Animals listen to their instincts, following their inner command and they reproduce in certain periods, but they do not enjoy it at all. However, people might lead a sexual life only for pleasure, not for reproduction. Other living beings reproduce in order to create the necessary conditions for the human beings' appearance and subsistence. But we are the only ones who can enjoy the body of another human being."

"Well… I have to admit that these examples might show that our aim is to enjoy the material world as much as possible, but still, I cannot believe that only this is the meaning of life…"

"You are right. There is something else that makes us different from animals."

"Is it the ability to create?"

"Yes. We believe that the aim of our existence is not only physical pleasure but spiritual joy as well."

"What do you mean?" I asked.

"The art. We are the only one among the living beings who are capable of admiring art pieces and enjoy the process of creation as well. And now, I do not mean instinctive art."

"Instinctive art? What is that?"

"It is a type of creation that is coded to many other living beings. Certain animals are capable of creating complex works which might have an artistic value, but because the animals are not conscious, they cannot admire their work. These animals create in order to survive, but they do not enjoy art."

I knew immediately what Yang was talking about: the wonderfully constructed nests, the geometrical beehives, the complex anthills or the great buildings of termites which work similarly to cities. Our scientists had never been able to give a convincing explanation to these phenomena...

“Therefore, this type of creative ability,” Yang continued, “is only an instinct like eating or reproduction, for instance. One of the main characteristics of human beings is that we are capable of enjoying everything that is only an instinct in other living beings. Art is not an exception either because, besides its original purpose, we can use it for amusement as well. That is why we create artistic works that are not necessary for the survival of our species: their only purpose is enjoyment. We could certainly live without paintings, sculptures, music and literature, but life would not be complete without them. We have an inner motivation to create and enjoy works of art.”

“And you believe this should not be the case, don’t you?” I asked.

“Why do you say this?” Yang asked.

“Well, you have told me recently about an unexpected error which caused a huge similarity between us and our creators…”

“No, I was talking about something else. Creative art is undoubtedly part of the original plan. It is not a mistake at all that we can enjoy art as much as physical pleasure. Otherwise, there is no essential difference between them. There is only one contrast between an artistic work and the human body: art pieces are inanimate, the human body is a living matter. Both of them are someone’s work: a nice painting, a good book or a catchy song is made by us, people, and we were made by our creators. This means that man is the most perfect piece of art!"

"But what were you talking about when you said that we began resembling our creators too much? What is the problem?" I asked.

"The problem is that we want to know how they did it."

"Make life?"

"Yes," Yang answered. "Every sign shows that curiosity should have never appeared. Our interest towards science does not fit into the picture."

"But why?"

"Think about it. They created us to enjoy the beauty of the material world as much as possible. What is more, they gave us the power to create in order to be able to appreciate the works that we have made, not only the things they designed for us. But instead of enjoying life we are constantly searching for the answer how they made everything. The aim of a man-made artwork is to give pleasure and not to make us think about how it has been created."

"This is true..." I agreed.

"So, our only task is to enjoy life, but curiosity ruins everything! This is the case in every civilization. It is a real tragedy when our interests towards science reach the point where we realize that we were created by someone. After this, we look at our life in a different way..."

"But why doesn't science fit into the picture?"

"It seemed to me that you have understood the problem when we talked about it earlier. You said that life was like a book, which we could really enjoy only if we did not know what it was about."

"Yes," I said. "But I do not understand why are you talking about science like it was a maleficent thing."

"Because it is a maleficent thing! The only aim of science is to reveal our creators' secrets. Biology, genetics, physics, chemistry, anatomy, astronomy: these are all meant to question them. And when this becomes the most important issue, our lives become senseless."

"I do not agree. First of all, we defeated diseases that used to be fatal by the means of science. If there were no science, the Earth would be a much worse place now. Second, not everyone is a scientist on the Earth, however, the great curiosity that you have mentioned is specific only to them."

"You are right," Yang said. "I have almost forgotten that you are not like the other civilizations. Your interest in science is not on the same level due to the ancient blending."

"Why? Is everyone a scientist on your planet?"

"Of course. We are very similar regarding our

physical and mental characteristics."

"Then you are all artists as well, right?"

"Yes."

"But is everyone familiar with each branch of art?"

"Yes, here everyone can paint pictures, compose music, create sculptures..."

"This must be very interesting!"

"I think you are more interesting," Yang replied. "How many people deal with science in your civilization?"

"Only a number of them."

"And art?"

"Not much more, either. For example, there are people who are excellent painters, however, they cannot play an instrument. There are people who know how to compose music, but they cannot paint. And there are people who can both compose and paint. So, there are several types of artists, but it does not happen often that a man is good at every branch of art. And to be a scientist as well—it is almost unimaginable. Of course, there are some examples of scientist-artists in the history, but only a few."

"I can conclude from this that there was at least one ancient civilization on your planet that was much more advanced than the ones with whom it blended. Those people who are equally good at art and science must be the descendants of that very advanced ancient species. But as you have said, it is more common on your planet that one gets one characteristic, the other gets other traits."

"But most of them get none," I added.

"Does this mean that most of the people on your planet are not interested either in science or in art?"

"Yes," I answered immediately, but as soon as I had said it, I realized it was not entirely true. I remembered those who are not appreciated by the so-called professional artists because, according to them, the works these amateurs create or love do not resemble "true" art. The music, pictures, sculptures, books made and loved by these people are considered to be too simple, meaningless and kitschy. But they are works of art, too. On second thought, there are many people who create but even more who enjoy such art pieces. Almost everyone likes some type of music, paintings, books, but usually not the same ones…

"Then, on your planet there are mostly people who enjoy various artistic works, but they are not interested in science, right?" Yang modified his question according to my previous thoughts.

"Yes, this is right."

"So, there are lots of people who lead their lives as our creators imagined!"

“But they cannot avoid poverty, wars and illnesses for example...”

“Yes, I have forgotten that. Again…” Yang said. “But you try to defeat diseases using science. And it is unbelievable!”

“Why?”

“It is just hard to accept the existence of a planet where science has advantages.”

“It may be strange to you,” I said. “But for me, it is hard to imagine a planet without wars, illnesses, starving children; where people live in perfect harmony and understanding. This kind of life could only be enjoyed. I agree with you that science has ruined everything on your planet.”

“Now you understand what the problem is in our opinion. Science does not fit into the picture. We believe that, according to the original plan, our only task is to enjoy the fruits of the creation: both our own works and the works of our creators.”

“And this can be achieved by the living energy, by our souls,” I added as to prove that I had been listening carefully since the beginning.

“Yes. Our soul comes from a non-material dimension. We exist there only in the form of living energy. Our creators designed a body in which we can feel the best possible, but now you also admit that they made a huge mistake. They did not assume that due to our emerging interest towards science, we would forget what the meaning of life is. Not to mention your planet, where this mistake is not the only one..."

Suddenly, a machine started beeping. Yang went there immediately and I, left alone, began thinking again.

Now it became completely clear that the most specific characteristic of the transitional period was the constant increase of interest towards science, i.e. the curiosity getting bigger and bigger. And the fact that on our planet there are both excellent scientists and people who are still led by their animal instincts, can be explained exclusively by the ancient blending.

According to Yang there had been at least one highly developed ancient human species that mixed with less advanced ones. And because we all possess some characteristics of every ancient human species that took part in blending, we are so diverse that we often say every person is a different world. However, these various people are able to cooperate, but unfortunately, mostly in cases they are fighting against someone or something...

Yang was still working on one of the machines, while I realized that I became much smarter during this short period of time. For instance, an hour ago it was a mystery for me how our ancestors could make such precise engineering works like the pyramids. But now I know that the ancient civilizations reached the level of advancement in which they could build such astonishing buildings easily, before the ancient blending happened.

And when the phase of blending reached them as well, it caused attenuation in their knowledge and genes. This is why all the legendary civilizations had become extinct.

Of course, this is not our fault. Our creators made mistakes. Inevitably, the question arises whether these faults could have been foreseen or whether these are faults at all. Yang told me that by doing this experiment they had made contact with approximately twenty other civilizations, but terrible things like wars, starvation and diseases appeared only on the Earth. The idea that our creators originally had not intended this kind of life for us pleased me.

According to the original plan, there should be peace on the Earth, people should have the same physical and mental abilities, and what is most important: we should live without hatred, wars and diseases. Is it a coincidence that most of the utopian theories and religions imagine ideal life in this way? Is it possible that our desire for equality and peace has deeper roots than we think? Somewhere deep inside we know exactly what the world should look like. What if our rebellion against inequality originates from another world?

After a few seconds of silence in my thoughts, I had to realize I almost forgot about something very important. It just looked like I was alive, but in fact, I was dead on my way to the afterlife. And then it occurred to me that a civilization which is capable of carrying out such an experiment, must have a more scientific opinion about the afterlife than we have. I was very curious how Yang's civilization imagined that place.

The only thing I had found out about the afterlife was that we were existing in a form of living energy there. However, only the concept of living energy was a novelty to me. I had heard many times that we go to the afterlife when we die, and according to this, the afterlife is probably the same place from where our souls arrived in our bodies. But then, why don't we have memories about the period before our birth?

I tried to remember all the information mentioned about the afterlife and the soul, and then it came to my mind that during our first conversation Yang mentioned that their greatest scientific success was the discovery of the materialized soul. I did not know what he was talking about and I could not ask him either, because I had just realized what the evolution was. But now I thought it was time to ask Yang about it. At the same time he turned towards me, so it was adequate to ask him the following question:

"Can you tell me about your greatest scientific discovery? About the materialized soul? What is it?"

"Yes, of course. The organ of the soul is undoubtedly our creators' most brilliant work."

"The organ of the soul?"

"Yes. We found direct evidence that we have souls and that the afterlife exists!"

– 9 –

"Until the discovery of the organ of the soul, we did not know for certain," Yang continued, "that we go to another place after death. Of course, we had suspicions, but we believed for long that the issues of soul and the afterlife would be similar to the meaning of life or the intelligent design: we "answered" these questions only by means of conclusions. And it seemed that there would never be a direct answer, but within a few years we succeeded in answering two major questions. First, we found the definite proof of our design..."

"The life seeds in the comets," I added.

"Yes. The second and our most important discovery was the organ of the soul, in other words the materialized soul, which proved the undeniable existence of the soul and the afterlife."

"This is unbelievable..."

"However, our answer to the meaning of life will always remain a guess because, as I have said it already, it is impossible to find physical evidence about the purpose of our creation or about our creators' will. So, if we had not discovered the organ of the soul, you would not be here now. It is the organ of the soul that helped us to switch to the passageway through which our souls travel to the afterlife."

"And where is this organ?"

"In the brain."

"How is it possible that we have not discovered it yet?" I wondered.

"It is not surprising at all. Our creators were very careful about hiding it forever! They hid it so well that it is not an exaggeration to say that its discovery was a bigger miracle than the organ of the soul itself."

"But how could they hide an organ?"

"Well, it is not like any other human organ. It is in fact just a small group of cells."

"So, we have not found it because of its size, right?"

"Yes. Don't imagine the soul cells like the size of an average brain cell. They are thousands of times smaller than any other cells! And not only their size but their function is also different from the cells which build our body."

"What is then the organ of the soul?" I asked excitedly.

"It is a tiny construction. In one of its half our soul is placed physically. When we die, the other half of the organ starts a process which opens a passageway to another dimension. After death our soul travels through this path to the afterlife."

"Afterlife is the same place where we came from at the beginning of our life, isn't it?"

"Yes," Yang answered. "The organ of the soul begins its function two times. Firstly, when we are around two years old and secondly, when we die."

"At the age of two?" I asked in surprise. "Does it not start its function when we are born, or even earlier, at the moment of conception?"

"No. It is true that our material existence begins with conception, but what would be the point of being conscious while we are a fetus? This part of the life is not enjoyable at all. This is why the organ of the soul opens its doors for the first time when we are about two years old. Only then can we get souls. Until then we behave exactly like animals: we are not conscious, however, our instincts work properly. Before the arrival of the soul we are not capable of real communication either. We can just imitate words that we have heard before. But at the moment when our soul arrives, speech and the ability to create our own thoughts begin to develop. From this point we have memories as well."

"I understand you. According to this, our soul must have been somewhere before it arrived into our body. Why don't we know anything about it?"

"Well, this is another question which we can only guess. But if we succeed in returning you from the afterlife, we will know everything about it."

"What kind of theories do you have?"

"Most probably, we do not have memories about the things happened before our arrival to our bodies, because we are designed to forget them. As we have already said, we exist in the material world in order to enjoy life as best as possible. But it has a very important precondition: we have to consider life as an only and unrepeatable possibility. It should be treated like precious treasure. And in order to achieve this, while we are alive we are not allowed to know that there is an afterlife and that we were created by someone. This can be accomplished both by not giving us the intellectual abilities which could lead to the discovery of the organ of the soul and by erasing our pre-body memories, or at least making them unreachable."

"I agree," I said. "Life has meaning only if we start it without memories."

"And regarding the lack of memories," Yang continued, "we have to admit that our creators did a great job. It was science which led us to the conclusion that there is afterlife, and not our pre-body memories. We could find the organ of the soul due to their biggest designing mistake: science. This also helped us in revealing a number of our creators' secrets, which caused a considerable decline in life enjoyment..."

"We got to the book analogy again, didn't we?" I asked.

"Yes," Yang said. "A writer can never read his own book as the people who read it for the first time. There is only one possibility to make the writer look at his book the way the others do..."

"...if every memory being the part of the writing process disappeared," I added.

"Exactly. If this happened, the writer would read his book as though he was reading it for the first time. He would enjoy every sentence!"

"Does this mean that we had more previous lives?"

"We do not know," Yang answered. "This is only an assumption. But it is a fact that there is a place from where we get into our bodies and do not remember anything about it. Thus, the only logical conclusion is that we were designed to act in this way."

"So, it is possible that we had more lives."

"Yes, it is. But there are other theories as well. Some think that we do not have pre-body memories, because this is our first life. These people believe that there are so many souls in the afterlife that not everybody can take turn even in billions of years. According to them, there are still lots of souls which have never lived in a body."

"But there is no possibility that one day I will live in my own body again, right?"

"Well, that's the thing: there is a possibility for that! The cells of the organ of the soul contain our unique DNA code like every other cell of our organism. We have proved that after our death this genetic information is also brought to the afterlife. This happens for a reason,

I am sure, but I do not want to make guesses based on this data..."

"But if I ever got my original body back, it would not be in the afterlife, right?"

"Of course not!" Yang said. "There is no matter in the afterlife. We do not have bodies there but we exist in a form of energy. Only our consciousness travels to the afterlife."

"But how can I meet my deceased loved ones and friends if we do not have bodies? How will we communicate, how will we see each other and how will we recognize each other at all?"

"The answer is very simple. Just think about it: at this moment we do not use our bodies or anything from the material world in order to have this conversation. Two consciousnesses are communicating with each other, not two bodies."

"This is true..."

"So, don't worry about the fact that you will not have a body in the afterlife. We can see without our eyes and we can hear without our ears. You experienced it every night..."

"Of course! The dreams!"

"That's right, dreams," Yang nodded. "The result of the dysfunction of the organ of the soul..."

"Is this also a mistake?"

"Well, I would not call it a designing mistake just an unexpected side-effect. However, the appearance of science is an absolute error. The organ of the soul is a brilliant mechanism, thus, it is unbelievable that those who had created it did not remember that the soul cells might begin behaving as any other cells."

"I do not understand."

"The cells of the organ of the soul started dividing. We believe this is our creators' biggest mistake. They had not assumed that putting the soul in the body would lead to the dividing of these special cells. Generation after generation their number is doubled. Every child has two times more soul cells than their parents do. We began resembling our creators too much due to this phenomenon. The more cells are in the organ of the soul, the more interested in science we will be, and the bigger possibility we will have to communicate by means of telepathy. If the number of the soul cells had remained the same as it was in the first generation of human beings, science would not have appeared in our lives!"

"This means that the scientists on the Earth have more soul cells than an average human being?" I asked.

"Yes. The ancient blending affected the quantity of the soul cells as well. If in the past only one human species would have appeared on your planet, now everyone would be on the same intellectual level. But more species developed, obviously not at the same time, and due to this people who appeared earlier had more soul cells. Later on, members of advanced civilizations mixed with those who were not at that level, and this caused a mix-up in the number of the soul cells. On your planet anyone can be born with whatever number of soul cells."

"This answers the question why the child of highly intellectual parents does not always have so good abilities," I thought.

"That is right. In our civilization the new generation is always a bit smarter than the previous one."

"But in some form this happens on our planet, too," I said. "Every generation has a number of scientists who put the whole humanity to a higher level by their work. However, on our planet the constantly developing science is not the only designing mistake. Hatred and animosity are also present due to the ancient blending. And this is a fatal combination, because we use the weapons made by modern science to destroy each other in the wars."

"This is a huge problem indeed," Yang said. Then he turned to a machine again in order to continue the preparation for the experiment.

This was the first time that I did not begin thinking immediately after finishing a conversation. The reason was not that I became tired but that I did not have so many questions as I had upon my arrival a few hours ago. Having found out great things, I had fewer and fewer questions. At that point, I was more curious to find out when I would continue my journey to the afterlife.

Anyway, I was sure I did not need to wait for long...

When I turned towards Yang, I realized that Yin was also in the room. I did not see when he had come in, he could have been there for a while. When he noticed I was looking at him, he said the following:

"We have just exchanged information about you. I am surprised that you succeeded in answering the question about what had gone wrong on your planet in the short period of time I was absent."

"Well yes, we have found the answer. But if you do not mind, I would like to ask when I will continue my journey to the afterlife."

"If your civilization was not so interesting, we could begin the experiment in a few minutes," Yin said.

"This means that I have to stay?"

"Yes... We would like to have as much information about you as possible."

"But how long will I be here?"

"For a few hours. Your soul can stay in this body until you fall asleep. As I have said, this will take a few hours at most."

"All right," I said while realizing that I became extremely relaxed.

– 10 –

“The most interesting thing for me is,” Yin began, “that science has advantages on your planet.”

“I completely understand you. After realizing how life should look like according to the original plan, I can easily put myself into your place. On your planet the scientific curiosity took away the meaning of life that would otherwise be nice and enjoyable, since here are no diseases, hatred, poverty and wars.”

“I am very sorry that things went so terribly on your planet. But you have to understand that this is an enormous novelty for us, thus we would like you to stay a little longer.”

“Of course, I understand it,” I said. “This also happens due to the curiosity that is a common characteristic of our civilizations. If nothing more, we are alike in this aspect. Otherwise, I also have questions, but I think I received the answer to the most important ones.”

“Yes, you are already familiar with our creators’ biggest secrets. But if you have further questions, feel free to ask."

"All right."

"Despite the numerous mistakes, your planet is definitely not a bad place in my opinion. For example, there are only a number of scientists, but their discoveries make everybody's life easier. Not to mention how beautiful the variety of flora and fauna might be."

"Well, it cannot be said that the Earth is a place where life could not be enjoyed and where everyone suffers. But unfortunately, it is also true that there are enormous inequalities and injustices. For instance, if someone has more money, he might have a better life..."

"Money?" Yin asked.

His unfamiliarity with the concept of money did not surprise me at all, after the fact that they had heard about wars and diseases also from me for the first time. So, I tried to explain what I was talking about:

"Money is an object with a specific value. Everything has price on our planet and we can buy anything for the right amount of money."

Yin remained silent.

"The only problem is," I continued, "that we must pay money in order to live a comfortable life, for the medicines against diseases, for water, food and clothes… We must pay money for everything."

Yin was still looking at me quietly, but as I had

finished explaining, he began asking questions:

"Maybe you are not capable of producing enough food and clothes for everyone?"

"Of course we are," I said. "We have enough of everything, but not everyone has the same amount of money. And the differences are not so slight: some people have more money than needed and some live in poverty."

"But why did you invent money then?"

I tried to remember the history of money in order to answer the question:

"Money came into existence by the replacement of barter. Before the appearance of money, our society looked like this: some people were good at shoe-making, some in pot-making, there were people who excelled in raising crops and others in producing food of animal origin... The point is that everybody needed these products, but only one or a maximum of two or three could have been made by one person. It was not just the fact that people had different talents, but time was a crucial factor as well. For one person it was impossible to deal with all the things at once. For a while, barter worked well. But because a wooden spoon was not worth as much as a sack of wheat, they had to specify the ratio between the values. It turned out very quickly that the most comfortable solution was to establish a common denominator. This is the story how money came into existence."

"Now I understand. The ancient blending explains the differences in money," Yin summed up.

"What? The ancient blending explains this, too?"

"Of course. You are not the same and this leads to the most natural consequence that not everyone has the same amount of money," Yin said. Then he went to Yang, who was still in the room working on a machine.

It is needless to say how shocked I was. Is the answer as simple as that? Not everyone has the same amount of money, because we do not have the same abilities. Does it mean that our feeling of the unjust differences in money is irrational?

Money had been created in order to give a common denominator to our products. And when I thought about it, I had to admit that it really was the most natural consequence that those people who had worked more, who had created more valuable products, had earned more money. And as we know, not only our genes but money is also inherited from generation to generation, thus, it is understandable that some people do not have to work at all due to their heritage from the ancestors, while others live in poverty. So, is this really the right explanation?

I do not think so. Due to some reasons we do feel injustice. Of course, many people think in many different ways. There are people who are just jealous. There are people who have everything, however, they are still working hard in order to gain more and more money. They feel injustice, because they are working themselves to death, but they do not have as much money as they want to. And of course, there are many people who want to have more money—but without much working. They also feel injustice, but these attitudes are apparently unfair.

Unfortunately, there are many people on the Earth who really live in injustice. For example, those people who are working decently, but have so low salaries that even their everyday needs are not always covered. The injustice could be seen best through the fact that in other countries these same people could lead a proper life by doing the same job. And those people who were born on a part of the Earth where only poverty and suffering are present, live in an extremely unfair situation. Even if they had money, they would not be capable of spending it, because there is nothing there to buy...

My final conclusion was that the consequence of ancient blending—the fact that we are so different in our abilities—could explain why we were so diverse in earning money. But still, there are enormous inequalities! I thought Yin was not right this time: it seemed to me that he had felt there was no injustice at all in the above mentioned facts. And because he appeared at the same minute in front of me, I began the conversation:

"The ancient blending can explain the difference in money, but you have to know that there are countries where people can lead a proper life from their salary doing a job, while in other countries, with the same job, the people do not earn enough money and they can hardly live from it. This kind of inequality is the real injustice, not only the fact that some of us have more money and others less!"

"Country?" Yin asked.

"Great... Another concept they do not understand..." I thought.

It was interesting how far we had got: at the very beginning Yin was the one who was afraid that we would not be able to communicate. He thought that he would be the one who would send me concepts that I could not understand. However, the opposite had happened…

I had told him the most important things about countries, and after that Yin said only a few words:

"I cannot believe it..."

"Why?" I asked.

"The division is so severe on your planet that you separate from each other even physically. This only deepens the differences."

"Yes, we know..." I said a little bit bored.

It seemed like Yin was surprised at my behavior. It might have been shocking new information for him, but not for us. We are all aware of the fact he mentioned. What is more, the division and the existence of countries are quite natural to us. We cannot even decide which happened first. Do we have countries because of the division, or we have division because of the countries?

All in all, I know the answer now. Both of them had been caused by the ancient blending.

"But why are some countries wealthier than others?" Yin asked.

"Well, the people who live in wealthier countries can relatively understand each other, so there is no crucial division among them which could cause decline in progress. But there are only a few of such countries. Most of the rich countries are the results of the good geographical status they have."

"What do you mean by this?"

"For example, some of the countries have a large amount of oil."

"What is that?"

"Don't you have oil deep underground?"

"No, we don't."

This surprised me well, because oil is a product of nature. It is not like countries or money that had been created by people. It made me think that they have not found out the existence of oil yet, and probably, they used some other kind of energy resource from the beginning.

"Do you know how oil came into existence on your

planet?" Yin asked.

"Of course," I answered. "Oil was formed from marine organisms that lived a long time ago. After their death, these plants, animals and unicellular beings had sunk to the seabed and after millions of years they transformed into an extremely high-energy organic material. We bring this liquid to the surface, because it is one of our most important energy resources. More precisely, the fuel produced from it."

"This is interesting!"

"But why don't you have oil?" I asked.

"Because the circumstances have never been adequate."

"Of course!" I said. "Here live and have lived fewer types of animals and plants than on the Earth."

"What is more, life appeared here only ten million years ago, so there was not enough time for oil to be formed," Yin added. "Maybe in one hundred million years... It is interesting that the appearance of oil on your planet is the result of the same mistake which caused the fatal diseases as well."

"Yes..." I admitted. "On the Earth most probably no one considered while refueling their car how strong and ancient the relation might be between gasoline and flu..."

"So, if I got it right, oil is the property of the country under which it can be found."

"Yes it is."

"And other countries can get oil only if they pay for it?"

"Yes."

"This is so unfair! Why didn't you conceive a better system?"

"Believe me, we were thinking about it a lot," I answered. "There were attempts to build more fair systems, but they all failed. And after the facts you have mentioned so far, I think I understand the cause of this."

"Because of the ancient blending."

"Yes," I agreed. "The consequence of the ancient blending is that we are all different, which is reflected in our thinking as well. Those social systems, which wanted to create an artificial equality, were destined to fail because they did not want to acknowledge that people were not the same. They based the whole system on the lie that everyone was the same. And due to the fact that it is not true, the systems which were aggressively trying to abolish the differences spent most of their time and energy to chase and eliminate those who were thinking in a different way. They obsessively wanted to build a system where everyone was equal, and they wanted to achieve this equality in the people's thinking as well. Maybe the worst was that they honestly believed they could succeed..."

"You are right," Yin said. "On a planet where

everybody is different, it is very hard to find a common denominator."

"Yes, it is hard, but still, we do have some common denominators. For instance, the human rights. However, they differ from country to country, so we cannot even say that we are entirely equal regarding the human rights. In some countries it works, but it does not work within the whole population."

"This is sad," Yin said with clearly visible signs of disappointment on his face. What is more, it seemed that he regretted the previous minutes. He probably thought that he should not have asked anything about us, because what he had heard so far caused him pain. But before I could say anything, he asked a question again:

"Are you sure that you tried everything to make your planet a better place?"

"I think we did," I answered. "Many of us believe that our current system, that we consider the best, is not the best at all, because it is full of injustice. But still, it seems that this is the best solution from several bad ones. Even now there are more systems on the Earth, but those are the best which do not try to make everyone the same but they respect that we are different. They allow everyone to do what they are the best in, and they let everyone think about the world whatever they want to. These are the best systems, even if money inequalities are present here as well."

"Is it sure that the money inequalities cannot be

prevented?" Yin asked.

"I think they cannot. There were several suggestions, but they failed even in theory. For instance, it seems fair if everybody earned the same amount of money. But the problem is that we are very different, so we would spend that money in different ways. Some would spend it on recreation, some would save it. We should not wait for long and money inequalities would appear again. In such seemingly fair systems poor and rich people would appear in ten years, even if everyone would get the same salary."

"This is logical," Yin admitted.

"Due to the fact that we are absolutely not alike," I continued, "the most natural consequence really is that money inequalities would appear sooner or later. There were suggestions which claimed that money should be erased which would be the most fair. Everyone would do their job, the thing they knew the best, and as a salary they would get all the products which were necessary for leading a proper life, but nothing more."

"And why did not you try this system in practice?"

"It might seem to be fair, but at the same time it would be the most unfair system!"

"Sorry?"

"Do not forget that we are all different," I said. "We are not like you, who possess the same physical and mental characteristics. On our planet the differences are huge, thus certain jobs could be only done by certain people..."

"I see," Yin disrupted me. "Some people would deal with light-work, others would have life-threatening or very exhausting jobs, but at the end everyone would get the same payment. This would be really unfair and it could not be achieved on your planet."

"True."

"However, our society works exactly like this. From time to time we divide the works, so no one can feel that he is treated unfairly."

"As I can see," I began, "a society can only be successful if it pays attention to its members' characteristics. This is why on the Earth the best countries are those which take into account the general truth that there are no two human beings that are exactly the same. An entirely fair system could be only achieved where everyone is exactly the same, or at least very similar. But the Earth is not such a place..."

"It is sad to know how crucial is the factor on which part of your planet is one born," Yin said. "One's life expectancy depends on it..."

"Unfortunately, this is true."

"But it is also sad that beyond division, hatred, wars and diseases, money is a problem that also affects the enjoyment of life."

For Yin this might have been a great realization, but for us it is a cliché: many of us have to choose money making instead of happiness. We try to obtain things constantly, and that little time which we get to enjoy life, disappears quickly.

We work hard, at the end of the day we arrive home tired and we have hardly any time to be with our loved ones. But sadly, we cannot live another type of lifestyle, because this is the system we created for ourselves. And the fact is that we cannot hope for better on our planet...

"I have to go now, but in a couple of minutes we can continue the conversation," Yin said and he went to Yang, and together they left the room a short time later.

I was left alone for a period of time, and I realized again that I hardly had any unanswered questions. I also thought that Yin and Yang had been told the most important things about my civilization. Of course, I did not exclude further answers and realizations, because there were still a few loose ends. But I did not think at all that my biggest realization was yet to come, and that there were only a few conversations left before it...

– 11 –

With regard to those particular loose ends, I remembered that in the other room another soul was waiting to continue its journey to the afterlife. They might have already begun the experiment... If that was the case, I wanted to know when Yin and Yang would try to bring it back. Maybe even during my stay?

I must say, I was very enthusiastic that I might see such a scientific breakthrough! Of course, I was aware that Yin and Yang had never succeeded in doing it so far, but theoretically, I had the chance to learn everything about the afterlife even before getting there. In that case I would probably have been the first soul which would have reached the afterlife as an already familiar place!

By the time Yin arrived, so I asked him:

"What about the experiment with the other soul?"

"It is over."

"Over?" I was surprised and a little bit disappointed. "Didn't you succeed in bringing it back from the afterlife?"

"We did not even try."

"Why?"

"It hardly understood anything we were saying. Probably, it was a soul of a child, or of an adult who was a member of a recently appeared civilization."

"I see..."

"Anyway, we can rarely stop a soul," Yin continued. "But to have two souls at the same time is extremely rare."

"Couldn't you talk about anything?"

"The soul sent only unconnected and meaningless images to our minds. But now it has returned to the passageway, and might already have gone through the best moments of its life."

"If you have mentioned it..." I began. "I am wondering what the aim of the life review is in your opinion. You know more than we do, I am sure."

"Yes, we know more, because you have not discovered the organ of the soul yet."

"This is true, but still, we are familiar with this phenomenon. Many people said that they had seen their life review when being near death, for instance, during an accident."

"This happens with us, too, but very rarely because there are not many accidents anymore."

"But what is then the most common cause of death

among you?" I asked.

"We do not live according to the default settings..."

"Yes, I know, but before you have switched over to live for a thousand years, how did you usually die?"

"In the way our creators designed it."

"Sorry?" I asked in surprise. "They designed death as well?"

"Of course," Yin said as it had been the most natural thing in the world. "They encoded death to appear when we were around eighty, and when our brain realized that our body was declining, i.e. that we would not be able to take care of ourselves anymore. Then our brain was supposed to stop the functioning of the body without any pain, while sleeping. Except for those people who lost their lives in accidents, everybody died in this manner here."

"Well… Only a few persons die in such a nice way on the Earth..."

"In our opinion," Yin continued, "only after our death should we see our first and only dream: the life review."

"So, this is why Yang has said that dreams are results of the dysfunction of the organ of the soul..." I thought.

"That is right. It just does not make any sense that we see unconnected images every night."

"But the life review is not a designing mistake,

right?"

"It is proven that it is not, because the organ of the soul collects the necessary memories throughout our lives."

"Really?"

"Yes. When the hormone responsible for happiness reaches a certain—in most cases very high—level, those memories that produced it are not stored only in the particular part of the brain but they are also copied to the organ of the soul. This is how the life review is made."

"The organ of the soul remembers when we were the happiest in our lives?"

"Exactly. But we do not know for sure what the main goal of this film is."

"But you have theories, right?"

"Of course. According to some, our life review reminds us of who the people in our lives were. It shows everything due to what it was worth living. The aim of the life review might be to prepare us for who we need to look for in the afterlife."

"Our creators believed that at the end of our lives we would forget who were important for us?" I asked skeptically.

"No. We think they expected that science would never be present in our lives. Don't forget that according to the original plan, we were supposed to stay on a less scientific level. They designed us to be incapable of creating photographs or films..."

"I see," I disrupted Yin. "If there were no photographs, the elder people could not remember so easily their grandparents for example. In about fifty-sixty years even the nicest memories fade. And we know it very well that before the appearance of the photo and video era, the memory of our loved ones lived on in our minds only..."

"That is right. This logical argument is the starting point of our most accepted theory. There is hardly any better explanation."

"But if the life review was created because of this, then it became unnecessary with the appearance of science. We are now able to make pictures and films by ourselves."

"I agree with this too. Making films is another ability that makes us too similar to our creators because, originally, this also used to be only their expertise..."

"And what other theories do you have about the function of the life review?"

"This is the best and the most probable one. Other theories are dubious. According to one, its aim is to soften the monotonous journey to the afterlife."

"In order not to be bored?" I asked with a smile on my face.

“Yes, but as I have said, this is not so probable. However, this theory also has a logical base. The transition of our soul from the material world to the non-material dimension probably takes some time. I do not think that it would be better to watch darkness only.”

“This is true...”

“So,” Yin continued, “we believe that the life review has the function of reminding and preparing us. Just think about it how big and sudden change would the afterlife be without this film! Imagine how confused you would be if you closed your eyes and fell in sleep in your bed at night, and instead of waking up the next day at the same place, you would find yourself in a different world where your deceased loved ones would be alive again...”

“This is true,” I said. “I was also confused in the beginning, even though I knew I was going to die.”

“You knew it?” Yin asked in surprise.

“Yes, because I was suffering from a fatal disease. I was in a stage where death was near. Honestly, I was waiting for it very much, because every minute of my last days were full of misery and pain.”

“It must be a horrible feeling to know death is coming,” Yin said and I think I saw sadness in his eyes. “According to the original plan, this should not happen even on the day when we go to sleep for the last time...”

Then he was just looking and listening quietly. I

thought he felt pity for me.

"But there is something I do not understand," I broke the silence. "Those people who had a near-death experience and saw their life review, claimed that it was very quick and short. However, my film was not at all like that. It was very realistic, and according to my estimation, it lasted at least for an hour when it was suddenly disrupted by you and I arrived to this body."

"Yes, we are familiar with this phenomenon," Yin said. "The same confusion in time can be observed during our dreams. It is the result of the unsuccessful transition between the two worlds."

"I do not understand this entirely."

"Well, due to the fact that you are dead, you know it for certain that our life review does not last for a few seconds. However, those people who began to watch their life review but they did not die eventually, felt it to be very short. The reason is that their soul began its journey to the afterlife, but it was not separated completely from the material world."

I immediately remembered what our scientists discovered about the dreams. They proved that in the physical reality our dreams lasted for a few seconds, however, we often felt that they lasted for five or six minutes, or even more.

"Yes, this is what I am talking about," Yin added. "The soul begins its journey, but it does not leave the body."

"So you say that we have a near-death experience every night?"

"Yes. During every sleep we almost die. This is a scientifically proven fact," said Yin, and we became silent for a few seconds.

By this time I realized another fact:

"You must be right," I said. "The dreams always begin when our brain activity becomes the slowest. In such cases the brain mistakenly thinks that we are going to die..."

"...so the organ of the soul begins the process of opening the passageway," Yin finished my sentence.

"Now I understand it! The life review begins in similar situations. During a seemingly fatal car accident for example, our organ of the soul also starts the process by mistake. But due to the fact that at the end we have not died, the film review seems to be very short, quick and very often it seems to be unconnected."

"Exactly like our dreams after we wake up," Yin added. "In most cases we forget them forever after a few minutes."

"So, our dreams have a direct connection with the life review?"

"Yes, we think so. As I have said, our creators designed death for everyone to come in the old age when we fell asleep and our organism stopped functioning. We believe that the life review should begin only then, during our last sleep. The fact that it happens other times as well, can only be explained by a dysfunction of the organ of the soul. We are sure that, according to the original plan, we should never dream."

"So, dreams are failed life reviews?" I asked.

"Yes, it seems. During our deepest sleep phase the passageway is only partially opened towards the afterlife, thus, the memories collected for the life review are mixed with our desires, fears, older memories and who knows with what else. The main work is undoubtedly the life review, so the dreams, which appear every night while we have a smaller near-death experience, can rightly be considered as a mistake."

"This all seems very logical and credible, but is it sure that our dreams are of no importance?" I asked. "On my planet many people think of them as something special..."

"Well, we had a theory before the discovery of the organ of the soul. Many of us thought then that we have been given the ability of dreaming with reason: in order to communicate with those who had already gone. But when we realized what the meaning of life was, we discarded that theory immediately."

"Yes," I said. "If we knew about the existence of the afterlife, we would live in a different way..."

"This is true, but my point has been that messages arriving from the afterlife are useless."

"Why?" I asked in astonishment. "Wouldn't it be easier for us if we could communicate with our deceased loved ones? If we knew for sure that we would meet them, and that there *is* life after death? I think this information would make life much easier!"

"And what could they tell us? They would probably say that we should not be sad because they are gone, and that we should enjoy every minute of life. Later on we would meet each other and then we would be capable of talking a lot. We could not do much else, because in the afterlife we do not have bodies."

"Well, on second thought, they could not say anything else that would be more useful," I admitted. "But still, I believe that our life would be much easier if we knew that our loved ones have not disappeared forever..."

"This information would definitely make our lives easier, but at the same time life would become less enjoyable."

"I know what you mean," I said. "But are you sure that life can be beautiful and enjoyable only if we do not know about the existence of our creators and afterlife? Believe me, I entirely understand that we can enjoy life only if we consider it as a never returning chance, but the loss of a close relative is such a tragedy that it can sometimes darken our entire life..."

"In my opinion, it is an exaggeration to think that mourning can darken our entire life," Yin said.

"However, if we remained in the way our creators designed us, we would accept the loss of someone much easier."

"What do you mean?"

"Originally, we were placed on an intellectual level which is enough to enjoy life and to create things by ourselves, but it is not enough to get to the realization that we were created by someone and to ask questions about our existence. If we had stayed on that primal level of consciousness, the loss of our loved ones would not cause such pain."

"I still do not understand you..."

"This is best described as a child's level of consciousness. Children enjoy life the most and they are capable of creating as well. However, we cannot talk about scientific development in their case. It would be painful to lose our loved ones at that intellectual level, but we know that children can move on relatively quickly."

"Well, in that way it really would be easier..." I admitted.

"The higher the level of consciousness, the more we are bound to each other and the loss of our loved ones is more painful."

At that point I was quiet for a while, because I was not sure if I understood everything correctly. So, I asked it directly:

"Does this mean that love is also a designing mistake?"

"Well..." Yin began. "Parental love is an instinct, and of course, it is part of the original plan. This was coded into the animals as well. Love, or in other words: great affection that went beyond instinct, is not a mistake according to one theory. It was probably encoded in order to ensure the survival of the human species. After all, we are our creators' most important work, so it is understandable why everything is done in order to keep our species alive. So, according to this theory, love is part of the original plan, and mourning is an unpleasant side effect that they might have counted with..."

"And the other theory?"

"According to that one, love beyond instinctive level is a mistake which also happened because of the unexpected division of cells of the organ of the soul. The advocates of this theory believe that our creators did not want to cause us pain willingly. They must have known that the strong emotional connections would lead to big problems sooner or later. The majority here thinks that love is also a designing mistake. I think the same."

"But these are all guesses, right? I cannot believe it…"

"Yes, these are only guesses. But why can't you accept that the excessive attachment can be an unforeseen mistake?"

"I accept it," I answered, "but I can hardly believe

that according to our creators' original purpose, we should be less attached to each other. Life was created to enjoy it and love is a beautiful feeling..."

"Sorry, you have to stay alone for a couple of minutes," Yin said and went away. I, as always, began thinking about the things I have just heard.

I quickly realized that it was not hard to accept that love was a designing mistake. But he was insensible when he said that it was an exaggeration to say that mourning can shadow an entire lifetime. It seemed as though he had not understood that our life would be much easier if we got at least one message from our loved ones from the afterlife...

On the Earth wars and diseases are the cause of many people's early death. However, on Yin and Yang's planet it is not an everyday phenomenon to lose a young relative or a friend. This might explain Yin's insensibility. I think he just forgot where I had come from. Again…

If everyone died on the Earth according to the original plan, we could endure grief more easily. Even if we did not know about the existence of the afterlife, we would much easily accept the natural way of life.

But sadly, on our planet almost nothing happens as it was designed by our creators. And death is not an exception either.

– 12 –

I had been waiting for at least ten minutes, when I realized again that I had hardly any questions. However, I remembered that I was getting closer and closer to the moment when I had to leave this body, and the thought itself helped me remember two of my previous questions immediately.

The first one was: how will I die? Or in other words: what will be my second death like? I thought they would probably put me to sleep because, as they said, my soul could stay in this body only while I was awake. But I could also imagine my second death as something more special...

My other question was about the afterlife. I was wondering if Yin and Yang knew or suspected something about it they had not told me so far. Of course, I was aware that they made this experiment in order to get information about that place, but I wanted to know how a much more advanced civilization imagined the afterlife.

What comes next when the life review ends? What

will we see? Maybe a dazzlingly white world with many clouds? Or an Earth-like place that would not be built of matter but our memories?

I have to admit, the multitude of unanswered questions made me feel good. I was glad that we would have topics to talk about. I had not waited for too long as Yin appeared after a few minutes. The conversation began:

"How will I leave this body? I would like to know what kind of death waits for me here."

"You will simply fall asleep and then your life review will begin."

"Will it start again from the beginning, or will it continue from the point where it was interrupted?"

"We do not know since we have never succeeded in having anyone back..."

"Will I get any medicine for sleeping?"

"No, we will wait until you fall asleep."

At that very moment something strange happened that had not taken place since I was in my new body. I yawned!

"As I can see we needn't wait for too long," Yin said and it seemed to me that he was smiling. But I did not smile at all! We could even say that I had a fear of death! This might sound strange, but I knew that falling into sleep equaled death, so it can be understood why I was afraid a little. After all, this is an instinct of survival. When we are in danger, the fear of death appears unconsciously. Fortunately, this feeling lasted only for a few seconds, so the conversation continued without any problems.

"But I am not sleepy at all," I referred to the yawning.

"Take your time, calm down."

"Don't take it personally, but I can hardly wait to go away."

"I understand you," Yin said and he went to the part of the room where I could not see him. However, I could hear him working on a machine.

Until now, I had been asking questions from Yin and Yang only when they were in front of me or looked at me. But this time, I felt experienced enough in the field of telepathy, so I asked my first question about the afterlife while I could not see Yin:

"Do you have any assumptions how we will find each other in the afterlife?"

"Yes, we do," he answered. "We believe that when the life review ends, you will reach a place that you liked very much, probably your home, and everyone who was important for you, who made you happy throughout your life, will be there. The organ of the soul collects these memories, and most likely, it will decide where and with whom you will begin your existence in the afterlife."

"And will we talk there with each other as we are doing it now? By way of thoughts without moving our lips?"

"We, the inhabitants of this planet, will communicate in this way, but you will not—at least not seemingly."

"What do you mean?"

"In our opinion, the afterlife is the copy, or in some way the continuation of our surroundings before death. That dimension is surely not like a concrete place here in the material world, for example this laboratory that everyone sees in the same way. All the souls from all the planets of the Universe get to that same place, but everyone sees it differently. They probably see it the way their planet, their cities and houses looked like. In this sense, communication will also be the same as it used to be during your life, but as I said, it will be the same only seemingly. The sounds leaving your throat cannot be real in a non-material dimension."

"Yes, I understand this," I said. "But how do you imagine the afterlife? As a place that is similar to the world of dreams?"

"We believe that it is more similar to the life review, because it is proven that it is part of the original plan. You could see how the life review differs from our dreams. It is no longer difficult to draw the appropriate conclusions."

"It is really not," I agreed. "If we look at the life review as the preparation for the afterlife, we already have the answer to how we should imagine the afterlife."

"Right," Yin sad.

"So, the afterlife is like dreaming but with one enormous difference: the picture is crystal clear and so realistic as if happening in the material world."

"Yes, we imagine the afterlife exactly in this way."

"Well, in the beginning of my life review this was what made me confused. First, I thought I was only dreaming, but the picture was too clear for a dream..."

"This also proves that dreams are absolutely useless," Yin said. "They just confuse us. Thus, the theory is logical that according to the original plan, only after death we should see without eyes and hear without ears for the first time. The life review is an excellent way of preparing us for the afterlife."

"And will we see the people there in the way they looked like during their life?"

"This is a theory as well, but according to the fact that we can identify the souls by the brainwaves, it is very likely that we will see everyone the way their external appearance was. However, we believe that our surroundings can be changed any time by the creative power of our thoughts. That is just scenery. Most probably, you will be able to create any kind of house you want. There are no material boundaries or physical laws."

"This is very interesting," I said. "But according to this, when I want to meet somebody I will just create them by way of my imagination?"

"No! We believe that we can create only the image of materials. However, the souls of the deceased people are not materials..."

"...but living energy," I ended his sentence.

"Exactly. And because the soul is independent and free, only a real relationship can appear between the deceased people's soul in the afterlife. You will not be able to communicate with an object created by you. We cannot imagine that apart from souls anything else might be able to create thoughts."

"And what about the time? Is there time in the afterlife?"

"Well, this is an interesting question. We can say that there is no time at all. At least, we cannot feel it, because we do not have the means. Afterlife is a non-material dimension, so there are no clocks with which we could measure the passage of time. Of course, we could create the image of a clock but it would be only part of the scenery. If you do not look at it, it will not work."

"This is very interesting, indeed" I said.

"But even a better example is our own body," Yin continued. "While we are alive, the passage of time can be best seen on the aging body. However, we do not have bodies in the afterlife. So, most probably, time exists in the afterlife, but there is nothing that could indicate it."

"In other words, we do not feel the passage of time there?"

"Probably. If you meet a person who passed away thirty years ago, he will not feel that he has not seen you for such a long time but only for a few days."

"This is strange but very logical," I said and we both remained silent for a while.

Then I remembered Yin saying at the beginning that it would not be worth dying if it turned out we had only one life. So, I referred back to that thought:

"If you succeed in your experiment and I bring the news that after death there is no way back, why wouldn't you like to reach the afterlife?"

"Well, it seems to be an interesting place, but we are afraid that it is uneventful and boring as well."

"Boring?" I asked.

"Yes. What do you think, why did they create the material world for us, and made it possible to live in a body?"

I was silent, so Yin answered his own question:

"Obviously to have experience we cannot have in the afterlife. Our civilization has decided that if it turns out there is only one life, we will not throw it away easily.

We will continuously put our souls into our clones in order to keep on living. But if it turns out that we can have several other lives, we will immediately go back and live according to the original plan. If for no other reason, then because we have not eaten well for hundreds of years..."

"I understand you entirely," I said. "But if we can have other lives, won't you be afraid that you would be born to Earth? I think we cannot choose the planet we would like to live on, because our creators designed life to be the same everywhere."

"You are right, I did not think of this at all..." Yin said and started thinking very carefully.

"Suppose we had hundreds of lives," I continued. "I think we would begin each one without memories, just like this one. So, what is the point of getting hundreds of bodies if we do not remember it at all?"

"If we have more lives," Yin began, "then the loss of memory probably lasts only until we get back to the afterlife. If we finally succeed in our experiment and bring you back, we will know whether you had previous lives, or this was your first one. If we had more lives, I think we would be able to remember and even compare them after death. This might be similar to an old man who considers his childhood, his academic years or any other period of his life as separate lives."

"I see what you mean," I said.

"So, the afterlife opens up a variety of possibilities.

Who knows, maybe we can even cast the roles among each other and decide who our parents or children will be in our next life."

"That would really be very interesting!"

"And I can say even more exciting things," Yin continued. "Let us imagine that this is everyone's first life and that this has been just a test."

"A test?"

"Yes. Let us assume that this human body is the first work of our creators, and when we have all finished with our lives, the experiences will be discussed in the afterlife. It can be imagined that we will design the next human body together, because the current one is not flawless. What is more, it is possible that we will not only need to replace the human body but also to design an entirely new material world with a different base..."

"Well, I could hardly wait to reach the afterlife!" I said enthusiastically. "Until now, I have been wondering if I will meet my loved ones, but after what I have just heard, I would also like to know if there will be some kind of continuation, or we will stay on the level of non-material existence forever."

"That is what this experiment is about."

"Well…" I added after a short period of time. "I really like the idea that we might design a new human body together. I would immediately make a suggestion: to make our teeth grow constantly during our whole life!"

The above was meant to be a joke, but Yin's face remained motionless.

"I have to leave again for a few minutes," he said and left. I was glad that I was again left with a lot of things to think about.

After the previous great realizations and answers this time I only heard a theory. But it entirely occupied my imagination. How great it would be, after finishing our lives, to be able to discuss the problems we had realized! And later on, we could create a new body, or an entire new world together. So far, I used to compare life to a book. And now, I have to add that there is definitely a need for a second, revised edition...

Undoubtedly, the most mistakes happened on the Earth, thus, we would be the main actors of the new designing process. The only problem of Yin and Yang's civilization—and as they told me, the only designing mistake on all of the other planets—is that the unexpected division of the soul cells brought curiosity and science which slowly but surely took away the meaning of life. This is a huge problem for sure, but unfortunately, there are much more terrible things than this on the Earth.

I think it is perfectly understandable why I was so excited about the idea of the second creation.

– 13 –

While I was waiting, I wondered whether the purpose of the possible second creation would be the same. Might the next human body's aim not only be life-enjoyment? And if there was going to be a new world, how would it differ from this one? Would it be arranged so well that the Universe could not be discovered even with the best telescopes? Anyway, did our creators design the Universe as well?

I was thinking about these questions when suddenly, I heard my inner voice:

"The creators of the Universe and the living beings could not be the same," Yin said, but I did not see him anywhere. "The matter has always existed, so the most that our creators could do was to use it according to their notion."

And then he appeared in the room.

"Do you think that the next human body will have a different function than it has now?" I asked.

"I do not think so. It is not hard to see that the life in

the material world has only one aim: to enjoy the fruits of the creation, i.e. the physical and mental pleasure."

"It is not hard, but it is not so easy either," I said. "When I heard about it for the first time, I could hardly accept it..."

"But why?"

"Well... maybe because on the Earth it is a luxury to enjoy life. Yes, if I think about it, this is the problem. On our planet only a few people live their life like it was designed by our creators."

"I see."

"On the Earth," I continued, "the life of most people consists of rare and short moments of joy. Only a few people can claim that they enjoy life continuously. Even the richest people can experience a tragedy, for example, in the form of a disease."

"And what are these small pleasures like?"

"For example, when we have a nice dinner with the one we love, or when we watch a good movie, when we listen to our favorite music, read an exciting book, when we drink a glass of good wine and of course when we have sex. We were created to enjoy these things throughout our lives, but on the Earth these moments are very rare and appreciated. Most probably it is not by accident that in these situations we think, and very often say out loud, that life is wonderful..."

"I see," Yin said. "Most of your life is not spent on pleasure but on constant fight. You fight against diseases, you work hard to earn money, but the saddest thing is that you fight against each other as well."

"This is why we appreciate those small pleasures," I said and I remembered something. Most of us do not enjoy life constantly, so we try to cure this situation on our own. With alcohol, drugs or with excessive eating, for instance. The psychologists associate this artificially produced happiness with the lack of real happiness. Our inner voice suggests us that something went wrong, because life is not as it should be. Is it possible that deep inside we are all aware that we were created in order to enjoy life? Or do we suspect it, at least?

"This is very interesting," Yin reacted to my thoughts. "And do you really feel well when happiness is created artificially?"

"Yes, but it does not last for long, and it causes more harm than benefit in the long run. Our goal is to generate pleasure for a short time, but we achieve just the opposite in the long run, because life in a body that is damaged by alcohol, drugs or enormous quantity of food is not so enjoyable. Not to mention that we become addicted after certain time, and then it is not about pleasure at all but merely about fulfilling the body's compulsive needs..."

Yin was looking at me quietly, so I continued:

"And now I see that even those people who

seemingly live according to the original plan, very often create artificial happiness. For example, it usually turns out that famous artists suffer from severe alcohol or drug addiction, even though they have a wonderful life. I do not think just about the money they have but that they are constantly creating! Still, it seems that many of them are unhappy..."

Yin was listening and paying attention carefully.

"Taking pleasure in artistic works and in the process of creating them is also part of the original plan, right?" I asked.

"Obviously."

"I would like to know how far art has developed here."

"Sorry?" Yin asked wonderingly.

"I am curious how much art can develop. For example, the film has recently appeared on my planet, but now we can create very realistic movies by computers..."

"That is not real art," Yin added.

"Not real?"

"No."

"What is it then?"

"A film is much more part of science than of art."

"Sorry?" I asked wonderingly.

"Yes, the film is science."

And then I remembered that Yin had said recently that film making was originally the ability of our creators only. I thought that he was talking just about the life review.

"Of course, films can be of artistic value," Yin continued. "But they cannot be compared to real art."

"And what is real art like?"

"It has nothing to do with science at all!"

Yin felt that I was confused, so he continued:

"Even the first human beings were capable of creating, because this ability was coded into us by our creators. Later on, with the unexpected progress of the organ of the soul, science appeared in our lives and it began to develop, influencing art as well. However, the most important characteristic of real art is that it does not develop at all."

"What do you mean?"

"Do you have ancient art pieces on your planet?"

"Of course," I answered. "We have statues and vases that are more than thousands of years old. We also have antique literature, centuries old paintings and compositions..."

"And can contemporary sculptors create more realistic or more beautiful statues than the artists who lived thousands of years ago?"

"Well, I would not say..."

"Then, according to this, art does not progress," Yin concluded.

"You are right..."

"The essence of art is that a work which is thousands of years old can be as enjoyable nowadays as it was in the time of its creation. However, this is not the case with science..."

"I see what you mean," I added. "For example, the first microscope is absolutely useless nowadays. And this could be said about other scientific achievements as well. Science does progress but art, evidently, does not."

"And this happens because art was coded willingly into us, unlike science that appeared due to a designing mistake. Other living beings have been given this ability to preserve their species, but we are the only ones who are capable of creating artistic works for others' and our own enjoyment. Every piece of art, from the first one to the last one, can be equally enjoyed. The passage of time does not affect them at all."

"So, if I understand it well, the film is not real art, because it can exist by means of science only?"

"Yes."

"This must be true," I agreed. "It can be said that the movies nowadays are much more enjoyable, the picture quality is better than it used to be. From this point of view, film is really more like science than art."

"I am glad you understand it. And there is another reason why a film cannot be considered as a piece of art: it is too perfect."

"Too perfect?"

"Yes. The film is nothing more but the creation of another world. It is the most perfect creation, because it resembles our thoughts the best. Essentially, creation is the expression of our thoughts in the material world. And the fact that we are capable of creating another world proves that we resemble our creators more and more..."

"You are right," I agreed.

"We were also first created in thoughts, because they needed to design us first. Later on, they created people from material as well."

"Thus, the film is a creating process at a higher level that we are not supposed to know according to our creators' original plan," I concluded.

"And this can be said about science as well," Yin added. "After all, our creators are the greatest scientists and the biggest artists at the same time. In order to create human body and any other living beings, science was needed. But they were excellent artists as well, because these creatures are very aesthetic. Just think about flowers, for instance. Every species could have been designed to be grey, but it did not happen in this way. Our creators took care to enjoy their view. Nature is an aesthetic masterpiece."

"I absolutely agree with you. Our creators are definitely the best scientists and the best artists at the same time."

"And we begin to resemble them more and more."

"Yes, I see," I said. "We begin to be too good scientists and artists."

"Of course, we are far from being as great as our creators are. However, we reached the level at which we do not spend our lives as we should..."

"Do you think that we will reach our creators' level one day?"

"I do not think so. For example, we had never succeeded in creating living matter. And when one of our first subjects, who was a member of a much more advanced civilization, said that they were not capable of doing it neither, we stopped trying. We can approach our creators' level only to be able to modify their work. Their greatness can be best seen that we can postpone our age to the highest level *they* set. We can only manipulate the living beings they created, but we are not capable of creating new forms of life," Yin finished and I yawned once again. "As I can see, you will leave soon," he said. "But there are two things I cannot understand about you and I would like to talk about it before you go."

"All right. We do not need to hurry, because I am not sleepy at all."

– 14 –

"The first thing I am unable to understand," Yin began, "is your belief about the origin of life. Despite your remarkable scientific discoveries, you still think that life appeared accidentally and that the Universe came into existence from nothing. I just cannot cope with this contradiction..."

"Don't forget that we have not discovered the life seeds yet," I said apologetically.

"It is not entirely true! You know about the life seeds, because you have found out that all the living beings on your planet can be traced back to one primitive microorganism."

"All right, this is true," I said. "I meant that we still do not have obvious, direct evidence since we could not have the opportunity to examine ice from comets yet."

"But the lack of that evidence should not lead to the conclusion that the first life forms appeared by accident! And this is what I do not understand. What are the facts that made you think that life had appeared accidentally?"

"I would like to emphasize," I said, "that there are people on the Earth who believe in intelligent design, however, only a few of them are scientists. The so-called evolutionary scientists spread the idea that life was caused by accidental processes."

"I am so curious what kind of argumentation could have led them to such a conclusion! How can one say that everything came into existence by accident, while having obvious signs of design?"

"I think," I began, "the main problem is that some regard it as obvious signs of design, but the evolutionary scientists do not do it so. I have always believed that life could not appear accidentally, and it led to the most natural conclusion that someone had designed it with some kind of purpose. Sadly, I have learned what the meaning of life is only now, when I am dead..."

"But the fact that we were created by someone can also be deduced," Yin said.

"It is true, but on the Earth until evidence is missing, no one will be entirely right. I am sure that on your planet everyone thought the same even before the discovery of the life seeds."

"Of course. And it is not strange at all that everyone believed the same, because there was only one obvious explanation. We were not surprised when this theory was proved with the discovery of the life seeds."

"There would be a lot of shocked faces on my planet!" I said with a smile. "I would like to know how the evolutionary scientists would react if the life seeds were discovered on the Earth. It would be a sensation when they found those certain genetic plans, among them the human DNA as a goal. It would definitely prove that life did not appear by accident."

"You say that on your planet this obvious fact would be accepted only when irrefutable evidence was found?"

"Yes. But if I think about it, it can easily happen that a number of our scientists would still claim that life appeared accidentally..."

"Sorry?"

"I think they would argue that the only evidence found was that the life seeds were in the ice of the comets, but it is unknown how they got there. So, the fact that the life seeds travel on the comets does not exclude the idea that they appeared by accident..."

"This is unbelievable!" Yin said. "But your scientists are the ones who discovered the evolution. They proved that the living beings appeared in a certain order."

"This is true. The only problem is that they made false assumptions and they do not want to admit their possible mistake."

"I cannot understand it! Every sign points to one direction and your scientists do not want to see it. If only our next subject was a scientist from your planet!"

"In my opinion, it would be a very interesting

conversation. You can be sure that he would make unbelievable theories about how he got here and about who you were. Most probably, you would spend all your time trying to convince him that he is not dreaming or hallucinating..."

"You think?"

"Yes, because the evolutionary scientists believe that the human beings are not the result of an intelligent design but of an accident. And the people who think this is the case, must also believe there is nothing after death and that our existence is aimless. The base of this ideology is nothing."

"Unbelievable..."

"Yes, it is," I agreed. "Another interesting fact about our scientists is that there is often a suspicion that they accept only those scientific facts as proofs which support their pre-formulated theories. However, science should not work in such way. It should not recognize only the evidence which fit into their theory, but a theory should be based on existing evidence."

"I can hardly believe it..."

"Of course, I do not underestimate the work of our scientists," I continued. "We owe a lot to them. But sadly, they often do not accept the obvious explanation and because of this, I believe, we resent them with right. It is true that on the Earth, at this moment, there is no unquestionable scientific evidence about the intelligent design, but of course, there is also no evidence that life appeared by accident. Both are theories only, but the evolutionary scientists believe in the less probable one."

"Yet I hoped I would get an explanation for this contradiction."

"Otherwise, I have never dealt in detail with the evolutionary scientists' theory about the origin of life, because I was sure that this theory, as many others, would crash one day. But since you have revealed that their assumption does not have a logical base, I am also more and more curious about the reason of this contradiction."

"What are those scientists like who claim that the human body became so complex and perfect by accident?" Yin asked, but obviously, this was a rhetorical question. "Imagine if the blood did not clot. Nothing could stop bleeding to death after a needle stick injury. And when we accidentally touch something hot, we pull our hands automatically. We do it so quickly that we realize only later what has happened. How could be this only an accident?"

"I am sure that our scientists have also asked this question, but still, they cling to their theory..."

"And not only the human body serves the proof for the intelligent design," Yin continued. "Let's see, for instance, the plants. It is impressive how amazing are the solutions our creators found to allow them to survive! Some of them bring tasty fruits which are consumed by animals, thus they take part in spreading the plants' seeds. Other plants have such seeds which with various tools, for example wing-like parts, reach far away. Is this also an accident?"

"When our scientists explain such phenomena," I said, "they often talk about animals and plants as highly intelligent and conscious beings. They say that plants *produce* delicious fruits in order to survive. Or that leaf bugs *choose* to resemble leaf shapes in order to *hide themselves* well among the leaves. And I have also heard that ants *produce* acid when attacked or that certain plants *protect* themselves with spikes. I have always smiled at the use of this self-revealing vocabulary."

"Isn't it obvious that delicious fruits were designed by someone who had known what other creatures would live on the planet, and what kind of taste and scent they would like?" Yin asked.

"I would never say that plants *know* what animals and people like, or that they know anything at all. Obviously, leaf bugs were designed by those who knew there would be leaves on the planet and what their shape and color would be. They knew because they were the ones who designed them as well."

"Exactly!" Yin agreed with me. "These tools were created in order to protect the living beings from extinction and to insecure species preservation. There are no such living beings which did not get something for helping their survival. The microorganisms got incredible toughness and the ability to double their number in a very short period. The plants have an enormous number of seeds, animals are able to accommodate to their environment, they have sensitive senses, some have hard bodies and there are many other solutions. However, the human beings have been given the best tool: consciousness! With this we are able to create any kind of equipment that exists in the nature, while other living beings can handle only their own tool."

"Yes..." I said. "How can we assume that animals and plants made themselves these tools? They have no idea that they are alive!"

Then we stopped talking for a few seconds, but soon I remembered a contradiction:

"I do not understand why our creators designed fruits which not any living being likes to consume. For instance, lemon: outside is bitter, inside is sour. It does not help in spreading its seeds at all."

Yin thought about it a little, but he remembered the explanation very quickly:

"This is also the consequence of the ancient blending. On our planet, where one evolutionary process happened, only those plants exist which produce delicious fruits."

"So, lemon is also a designing mistake?"

"Yes, it is. As we have found out earlier, the mixing of differently developed human species originating from more evolutions resulted in the appearance of a blended species that is very different from our creators' will. And this is also the case with lemon. Not only human species were affected by the ancient blending but animals and plants as well. This is the reason why the lemon did not become as previously designed. Sadly, this might be an everyday phenomenon on your planet, since you have millions of plant and animal species. We have only three thousand, but they all resemble our creators' will. Their only one aim is to serve people."

"Well, we have many plants which are threatening people and other living beings," I said. "I would not say that they serve us…"

"Life-threatening plants?"

"Yes. We have a lot of poisonous plants. And there are many dangerous animal species as well."

And then, I remembered that the same contradiction occurred to me earlier. It was then that I understood that, theoretically, every living being existed in order to serve the people but lions, for instance, were out of the picture. And there are many other animals which live at the same time with us, however, they have nothing to do with us.

"Now you know the explanation," Yin said when he heard my thoughts.

"Yes. The ancient blending…

"This is why you have many plant and animal species which do not serve people at all."

"Does this mean that we need around three thousand species only?"

"Yes. Our flora and fauna works perfectly with this number of species."

"So, you do not have any plants or animals that are threatening people, right?"

"Right. Why would our creators put us into danger?"

"Good question..." I thought to myself.

"And there are no life-threatening microorganisms either," he added, referring to the diseases that exist on our planet only.

"What to say… It seems that our creators designed a world that could not be nicer. In this world there are no diseases, hatred and wars. And the living beings that live on the planet are not dangerous at all. Everyone has very similar physical and mental characteristics and our only task is to enjoy the physical and mental pleasures as much as possible. Even our death is designed to be the most beautiful..."

"The plan was very good," Yin said. "And if we ignore the mistakes, we can say that the realization was also brilliant. However, your scientists do not see the signs of the intelligent design..."

"Only the evolutionary scientists..." I corrected Yin. "I have to remind you that we have scientists who believe in the creation."

Then I yawned and I felt for the first time that I was getting sleepy. I knew I could not stay for long, and because Yin said that he had two things about us that he did not understand, I asked him what the other one was.

"It is not so important," he answered. "If you want, I will leave you alone so that you can sleep. There are just the last preparations left in order to begin the experiment."

"But I am not so sleepy. So, what is the second thing?"

"Well, I do not understand how you knew about the existence of the afterlife. When we talked for the first time, and I said that the aim of this experiment was to find out everything about the afterlife, you were not surprised at all. Our subjects, who were at a similar level of advancement as you, heard about the afterlife for the first time from us. But you had known it already. First, I thought you knew it because you had also discovered the organ of the soul, but it was quickly revealed that you were not member of a so advanced civilization as it seemed in the first minutes. It is still strange to me that you already knew where you would get after death."

"Well, I was very surprised that I found myself on another planet, in another body but yes, you are right, I knew about the existence of the afterlife. Or at least, I suspected it."

"And this is what I do not understand! How do you know about the existence of that non-material dimension without the discovery of the organ of the soul? How did you get to know about it?"

"We did not need to discover anything. People have believed in the creation and in the afterlife for thousands of years."

"Sorry? For thousands of years?" Yin asked in astonishment.

"Of course," I answered and I yawned again. "Every important world religion is about it..."

"Religion? What is it?"

"Well, religion is in fact the acceptance of the idea that we did not appear by accident but that we were created by someone and that there is afterlife."

"A thousands of years old scientific theory that is based on no evidence?"

"Well… yes. On the Earth whoever believes in this without any scientific evidence is considered to be a religious man."

"This is unbelievable!" Yin said. "But how did you get to these scientific conclusions thousands of years ago?"

"This is an interesting story," I said. "The church and the religious people believe that this information was communicated to us by the Creator himself. The Bible tells many stories in which God made contact with the people..."

"What? You have met our creators? Why do you say this only now?!" Yin asked with the apparent signs of dismay on his face.

– 15 –

"I have not talked about religion so far," I answered, "because you are members of a much more advanced civilization, and in my opinion, religion is not scientific at all."

"But why didn't you mention that our creators had contacted you?!" Yin asked still being shocked.

"Because it is not sure that it is true."

"Sorry?"

"The Bible that writes about this alleged contact," I began, "is in fact a book full of strange imagery and stories that are difficult to interpret. These narratives, which are thought by many to be made-up, are undoubtedly educational: they give moral guidance and they are unavoidable parts of the human culture. But we cannot believe every word of that book, because most of the stories are hardly understandable, and we can read about many things which were obviously created by human imagination. The point is that it is not sure at all that our creators visited us. It might turn out that the whole Bible is just fiction. This is why I thought that it was unnecessary to mention."

"How can this be unnecessary? If it is true, then you are the only civilization in the Universe we know our creators have contacted! And you mention it only now, when there is barely any time left till your departure..."

"I understand your anger," I said. "But even if I had begun with this, I could not have told you much. The Bible is a lengthy book, but I know only a few stories. And if I had begun telling them, you would have recognized quickly that I was right, because they make not much sense at all..."

"But still, what are the stories like?" Yin urged me.

"Well, there is one about the alleged first human couple, Adam and Eve. They lived in the Garden of Eden and God told them that they could eat fruits from each tree, except the tree of knowledge. However, they ate it, thus, God expelled them from the Garden of Eden. According to the Bible, this is the cause of every bad thing which has happened to people ever since..."

"But what was the Garden of Eden?"

"You see, this is what I am talking about!" I said. "These stories cannot be interpreted word by word. This is why we give them symbolic meanings, and in this way, many interpretations are possible."

"Can the Garden of Eden be the symbol of a joyful life?"

"Of course it can," I answered and yawned again.

"And if I understood it well, all the problems began when the first couple ate fruits from the tree of knowledge despite the ban?"

"Right."

Yin became silent for a few seconds, and later on, he said only the following:

"This is unbelievable!"

I waited for him to add something, but he was only looking at me distractedly in silence. I must have been very sleepy, so I did not have the slightest idea that the biggest revelation of my life was ahead.

"You have had physical evidence about the meaning of life for thousands of years!" Yin said. "This is incredible! We have thought that there cannot be physical evidence about our creators' will, but now it turns out that you possess it!"

"What?"

"When our creators contacted you, they told you they designed life in order to enjoy it at most. This is what the Garden of Eden is about. And they also warned you that curiosity, the thirst for knowledge, would destroy everything! The tree of knowledge must be the symbol of science! They told you that science was the forbidden fruit. You have known for thousands of years that science takes away the meaning of life!"

"This is really unbelievable," I said and I finally understood the importance of the previous sentences. I could hardly believe that everything this advanced civilization had told me about the meaning of life was nothing more than one of the widely known stories of the Bible.

"I am sure that now it is easy for you to realize why it is hard to interpret the story," Yin said. "It is not surprising that the message of our creators appeared in the people's head in a very picturesque way..."

"Of course! The communication based on telepathy does not work in a proper way if one of the partners' knowledge is incomplete! I have experienced it in the previous hours."

"Right," Yin approved.

"It is obvious that we could not understand everything they told us during our encounter."

"And the things you did not understand," Yin added, "appeared as strange pictures in your minds. This is the way ancient texts were written. If your civilization was on the same level now as it was then, you would not understand me so well either."

"This is true..." I said and Yin ran out of the room.

While I was waiting, I remembered that the word Eden meant delight, so the Garden of Eden must refer to a place where physical and mental pleasure could be enjoyed. Our creators made it clear that life would be so nice only if we did not begin to deal with science. This has always been present on the first pages of this widely known book...

Obviously, it was my most important realization. I was shocked and I was under the influence of this discovery for long. A few minutes ago I was almost asleep, but now, I felt like somebody threw a glass of cold water into my face.

By the time Yin came back with Yang.

"It was not our creators who visited you," Yang said confidently.

"Why do you say this?" I asked in astonishment.

"Because once we succeeded in stopping a soul which had been a member of a traveling civilization."

"A traveling civilization?"

"Yes. A planet may become uninhabitable, and until the inhabitants find a new home, they live on spaceships. Maybe such kind of civilization visited you. And I have another reason to suspect that it was not our creators who visited the Earth."

"And what is it?" I asked.

"In my opinion, it is not probable that our creators would reveal their existence. By doing this they would take away from us the meaning of life. But let us assume that they visited you. Seeing there were diseases on your planet, they would have encouraged you to deal with science because it could help you. They should have advised you to eat the fruits of the tree of knowledge! So, it is more logical that not our creators but members of another—more advanced—civilization visited you and shared their knowledge with you. They told you everything they had discovered in the same way as we did in the previous hours."

"I have to admit you may be right..." I said.

"It just does not make any sense," Yang continued, "that our creators contacted you and told you why people had been created. For me, it is absolutely unimaginable that they would visit each planet in order to inform the civilizations to avoid science..."

"You may be right..."

"So, probably the members of another civilization contacted you and they tried to tell you their bad experiences," Yin added.

"Yes, this might be so," I said and yawned again.

"And what other stories can be found in the Bible?" Yang asked.

"Well, I have already said that I do not know much, but there is an interesting story about the creation of life. And now, when I think about it, the story is in fact about evolution. Of course, without the use of this particular word..."

"Sorry?" Yin asked. "How could the people

understand what the members of the more advanced civilization were saying about the evolution?"

"It was very picturesque," I answered. "According to the story, the creation of the world lasted for six days. Not even God was able to create everything in a second. For example, the first living beings, the plants, appeared on the third day. On the fifth day God created the aquatic, on the sixth day the terrestrial animals and people were the last one."

"Incredible..." Yin said.

"There are people who interpret this word by word," I continued, "and they really believe that the world and the life were created in six days. Others believe that the six days represent six eras, six different stages."

"Anyway, the sequence is perfect!" Yang concluded.

"Yes," I agreed. "Since we have discovered the evolution, we found it very interesting that people even thousands of years ago knew that the living beings did not appear at the same time but in a certain order."

"They did not know it, somebody told them," Yin corrected me. "Without scientific knowledge it is impossible to find out that in the distant past the aquatic animals appeared first and only later came the terrestrial ones. Or that the last step in the evolution was the appearance of human beings. That book is not fiction, I am sure! A less advanced civilization cannot find out such facts!"

"I agree," I said and I realized that I was getting more and more sleepy.

"And what about the evolutionary scientists? How do they explain that the Bible also claims that there was a specific order in the appearance of living beings?" Yin asked.

"They say this is only a coincidence."

"I could have guessed it... Is there anything else about the evolution in that book?"

"Yes, there is," I answered. "When every living being appeared, our creators told us to rule the animals. And this refers to the same fact you have told me about the evolution: all the other living beings exist only to ensure our living conditions."

"This is unbelievable..." Yin said.

"Is there something about the creation of the human beings?" Yang asked.

"There is a reference that we were created from the dust of the earth."

"Yes, they probably tried to explain that the human body consisted of the same materials as anything else in the world."

"This is also an argument that members of a more advanced civilization contacted you," Yin said. "The people who lived then could not know that our body consisted of the same chemical elements as the earth."

"Yes, now it is clear that the contact mentioned in the Bible had happened for sure," I said. "It can be also read in the book, and religious people often mention it, that God created man in his own image and likeness. Humans are the only living beings that were created in this way, so even the Bible makes difference between people and every other living being."

"Our soul is the difference..." Yang said.

"At that time, the members of your civilization were not developed enough to understand what they heard from the more developed visitors," Yin said. "You will understand what the Bible is really about only in the future. A few generations later, when telepathy appears, you will understand how the visitors communicated with you..."

"Yes, probably it will happen in this way," I said while yawning again.

"Anyway, it is incredible that there are written memories about this ancient meeting," Yang added. "But it is not so surprising, because such a contact must have left a deep impression in the people who lived then. Just think of the spaceships which landed on the Earth…"

"This can also be found in the Bible," I added. "Of course, they were not mentioned as spaceships, because the people had no idea what they had seen. In the Bible, and in other religious texts as well, we can find many examples of vehicles by which gods travelled between the earth and the sky. This has left a very deep impression in humanity, indeed. Major organizations cherish the memory of this encounter."

"What do you mean?" Yang asked.

"The church. We have temples all over the world. These are buildings where religious people go in order to listen to priests reading stories from the Bible and try to interpret them in a correct way."

"So, if I understand it right, the people who go to church believe that we were created by someone?" Yang asked.

"Right. And they also believe that their soul will reach the afterlife when they die."

"Do you know how many people are religious in your civilization?"

"The majority believes in some kind of higher power," I answered. "Not everyone goes to church, but many people believe in creation and in the afterlife."

"Except your scientists!" Yin added.

"Well, yes..." I said. "There is a huge gap between the church and the science. The scientists want to prove that there was no creation and that life appeared by accident..."

"Here just the opposite is true!" Yin said. "The discoveries made by the scientists led us to believe that there was creation and that we are the result of an intelligent design."

"And why is there such a big gap between the science and the church?" Yang asked.

"There is a reason for that," I said and I yawned so long as never before.

"Can you tell us something more about it?" Yang asked.

"Of course."

– 16 –

"In my opinion, the relationship between the scientists and the church worsened when the development of science reached a certain point," I began. "Earlier, the church was the only one who had a theory how the world, life and people had appeared. That idea was, of course, built on the writings found in the Bible. In other words, everything was based on what our ancestors, who had no scientific knowledge, heard from the members of a much more advanced civilization which visited us. The church even created the image of our creator. They said that a bearded old man lived in the clouds watching us constantly. However, after certain time, scientists refuted this idea by means of telescopes..."

"And was this enough to declare there had not been any creation?" Yin asked in astonishment. "The scientists only proved that the church had imagined something wrong."

"This is right," I said. "However, it is easy to judge with the science used nowadays..."

"But still, this reason is not enough to proclaim that there is no creator and that there has never been any creation at all," Yang said.

"So, why is there such a huge discord between the science and the church?" Yin asked, but before answering it I yawned again.

"First of all, the church did not want to accept the results of the scientific research which refuted many of their ideas," I said. "They were clinging to their theories and they were ready to do even the most terrible things in order to silence the scientists who claimed something else."

"Did they do this only because the results of the scientific research differed from their point of view that was based on ambiguous texts in the Bible?" Yang asked.

"Yes," I answered. "It is very interesting that the church was against the theory of evolution, even though the Bible says that the living beings appeared in a certain order..."

"This is unbelievable!" Yin said. "So, they did not want to accept the facts discovered by the scientists that already existed in the Bible, right?"

"Well, the truth is that the church had the most problems with the statement that humans originate from animals. However, scientists made a huge mistake as well. They drew an incorrect conclusion based on the fact of the evolution: they said that there was no creation. And they cling to this idea as stubbornly as the church clings to their idea."

"But why?" Yin asked.

"I do not know... It is certain that our scientists' claim—that life appeared by accident—is not based on facts, because there are no such facts at all! They have never succeeded in creating living cells by mixing inanimate materials randomly in laboratory conditions."

"And they never will," Yin said.

"Sometimes," I continued, "I feel that scientists cannot forgive the church that their predecessors were sent to the bonfire hundreds of years ago. It is a terrible assumption, but it is as if the scientists removed the creation from their worldview because of a petty revenge..." I finished my sentence and I realized that I could hardly keep my eyes open.

"As I can see, you will not stay here for long. Now, we will go and do the last preparations for the experiment," Yin said.

"But will you come back?"

"Yes, we will," Yang answered and they both left.

In the next few minutes, while I was trying hard not to fall asleep, I remembered those people who believed the scientists and rejected the idea of creation and the existence of the afterlife. I felt sorry for them, because they can hardly accept the death of their loved ones and friends. It can also be seen from this example that how dangerous science is.

The scientific worldview made the lives of many people empty. The evolutionary scientists caused many people to believe that they came into existence from nothing and that after death nothing awaited them. Their life became harder, because the scientists suggested that if someone died, then they would *never* meet them, they lost them *forever*.

And because it is not easy to accept this, grief often makes people sick. But if we believed that there was a continuation after death and that we would meet our deceased loved ones again, we could live a better life even on the Earth.

Our civilization has a great advantage compared to others: we have known this for a very long time. As it turned out, the civilization of Yin and Yang discovered the existence of the afterlife only by means of scientific research. But we had known about it for thousands of years. Of course, it is another issue that, despite this knowledge, many people on the Earth still believe in nothing or in coincidence...

In the meantime, I yawned more and more and was getting sleepy. I was sure that I had only a few minutes left until I would be closing my eyes forever. Yin and Yang promised they would come back. I believed they might say goodbye. I did not know how long they would be away, but I wanted to say goodbye before my leaving.

– 17 –

I was still waiting and I became so sleepy that I began to accept the possibility I would leave without saying goodbye. And since all of my questions were answered, my head was completely empty.

I did not regret the few hours spent on Yin and Yang's planet at all, but I was looking forward to meeting my deceased loved ones and friends again. And finally, when I almost fell asleep, Yin and Yang appeared in the room.

"Everything is ready for the experiment," Yin said.

"Do you see any chance that you will succeed now?" I asked while yawning.

"Sadly, it seems that everything will happen as it has each time so far..." Yang answered.

"But sooner or later we will understand the cause of our continuous failure, and then we will succeed for sure," Yin added.

"So, is this only a matter of time?"

"In my opinion, it is," Yin answered.

"And you have much of it..." I remarked.

"However, the chances are great," Yin said, "that this experiment will never be successful. As we know, we are born without memories, so it is possible that each time when a soul reaches the material world, the memories are automatically lost. And if this is indeed the case, then it is useless to bring either you or anyone else back, because you will not remember anything you learned in the afterlife."

"And what will you do if this is true?"

"Then nothing remains but to start living the life our creators designed for us: to enjoy it at most and to get familiar with the afterlife only when the time comes," Yin answered.

"Maybe it would be the best solution," I said. "So, is there a possibility for us to meet in the afterlife?"

"Of course," Yang answered.

"I can hardly wait to be there," I said. "You know, when you stopped me I was angry with you, because I was afraid that due to your intervention I would never reach the afterlife. But now, before my second death, I am grateful that I can die according to our creators' original plan. My first death was very ugly, you could not even imagine it. But at least, my second death will be nice. I will just fall asleep and reach the afterlife without any pain or suffering."

Yin and Yang were silent.

"Some of the people who had a near-death experience," I continued, "said that they were so close to the afterlife that they could see their deceased loved ones, who were waiting at the end of a tunnel. I am so curious if this is really the case."

"You will know it shortly," Yin said and I think I saw envy on his face.

All in all, I could hardly keep my eyes open, so Yin and Yang said goodbye quickly.

"It is time to leave you alone," Yin said.

"Yes, I think it as well," I agreed.

"We hope that our experiment will be successful and that we will meet again shortly," Yang said.

"But if it fails, we will meet anyway—but on the other side," I said with a smile on my face.

Then both of them turned and left the room.

After that I remembered everything I had heard from Yin and Yang in the previous hours. The strangest thing was that they had not told me much new. They just put the pieces in the right place and made me recognize the connections.

Of course, we are still short with a few scientific discoveries, however, we had suspected for a long time that something went terribly wrong on the Earth. Many of us feel deep inside that life should be nicer and happier. As if an inner voice keeps suggesting that hatred, wars, diseases and poverty do not fit into the picture. This is the reason why many people question the existence of our creators: it is hard to imagine that they intended these horrible things to happen to us...

At this point it was clear that I would be sleeping in a few seconds, so I closed my eyes, and I believe, I fell asleep with a smile on my face.

– 18 –

The first thought after my second death was that I had never been so relaxed before.

I suffered from a fatal disease, so death did not surprise me when it came a few hours ago. However, I did not realize immediately what was happening. But now it was a different situation: there were no doubts that I was dead. And because it was my second death on the same day, I paid attention to completely different things from those after the first one.

For instance, this time I was much more aware how quickly our physical and mental tiredness disappeared when death had come. Just a few seconds ago I could hardly keep my eyes open, but now I was so watchful that I could neither close my eyes nor wink. Of course, it was not surprising at all, because after a few hour break I again did not *see* things with my eyes...

I felt like the reader of the several times mentioned book analogy, who was already familiar with the plot... The reason for this was that my life review started from the beginning, and not from where Yin and Yang's experiment had interrupted it. In practice, this meant that I had to wait approximately one hour* in order to reach the part where the film had suddenly stopped after my first death. I knew exactly what I would see in the next sixty minutes, thus, the first twenty scenes of my life review could not grab my attention at all...

I cannot say that I was completely indifferent to the screening. The scenes softened my heart for the second time as well, however, now I was not so moved as I was for the first time. I watched, or better to say, I relived again the family idyll from my infancy, the film's opening scene, and then my memories from Christmas when I was around three. Everything appeared in the same order. And because I had seen these shorter-longer scenes a few hours earlier, my thoughts wandered unwillingly. Of course, I did not remember any questions but I did remember Yang's words: we would not enjoy life so much as soon as we found out its meaning. And that particular book analogy could have been a film analogy as well, because I felt this was also true for the life review.

A few minutes later, it came to my mind that during the first screening I had been waiting very excitedly for my first kiss. The initial shock was over by then, and I had already accepted the fact of my death. I had enjoyed what I saw, but now I realized that my attention slackened by the passage of time. What is more, I did not enjoy my life review at all. At that moment, there were two other things that interested me more than the things I was just watching.

First of all, I was looking forward to the part where my life review was disrupted after my first death. I was curious to find out what would happen after reaching my first summer vacation, the moment when my mother's sentence was interrupted and the picture suddenly disappeared. I think this is how the projectionists felt after they glued a torn film roll. They knew exactly where the film had torn during the previous screening, thus, they were waiting impatiently to see if something would happen at that certain part.

Most probably, they were afraid that the film was not glued perfectly and the roll might tear again. Or they remembered that gluing could have some consequence what the spectators might realize. I was also suspecting the latter: I was wondering whether something would happen at that certain point.

But of course, I was much more excited what would happen at the end of the film. After the conversations with Yin and Yang, I became very curious to find out what kind of a place the afterlife might be.

Due to the fact that they shared all of their discoveries and theories with me, I was—in a certain sense—equal to them, because I also had only one unanswered question left. And I must admit it made me happy that I would get the answer before them. However, I was very sad at the same time, because I could not enjoy the life review—this brilliantly composed and moving work of our creators'...

After a seemingly long wait, the film finally reached the point where I was on my first summer vacation at the sea. I knew: the part, where the screening had been disrupted for the first time, was very close.

A few minutes later my mother began oiling my back, and that very sentence continued as easily as nothing had happened previously. I did not see any indication that a few hours earlier, at this same point, something very strange had happened to me and to the film.

My nicest moments continued and I was very happy because, finally, I saw new scenes! After I had relived my success on the first performance with the school orchestra, my first kiss began. And in order to enjoy it the best, I willingly suppressed the wish to find out as soon as possible what would happen after the end of the life review.

But sadly, I became disappointed because the experience was not at all as expected. I did not have to think much to realize what was missing: the tingle in my body.

Of course, I was aware of the fact that I did not have a body, but it seems that I forgot about it from time to time. The first kiss was my first experience that reminded me of this very effectively.

After this minor disappointment, the newer scenes provided me some comfort. However, as I was traveling forward in time, their number decreased, or to be more precise, the time gap between the memories grew. I realized that after the years spent on college, the period between two happy moments was first more weeks, then more months, and in the years before my tragic death even a year passed between two scenes.

I do not consider my death to be a tragic one because a rapidly developing and a very severe disease killed me—but because I was only thirty years old when it happened.

There was nothing in the life review after my diagnosis, precisely, about my last six months. The last scene showed an event which had happened more than a year before my death. It was my last birthday that my grandmother was still with us. She died two months later, however, we did not suspect that she would leave soon, despite her old age. And of course we did not suspect that this was my penultimate birthday either. I spent my last one, the thirtieth, in the hospital and I died a month after that.

Nothing special happened on my 29th birthday: my family was together and we had a good time. I did not understand why this event had such a special place in my life review. My first kiss lasted only for a minute and a half, but this birthday party took place for a very long time. I felt that it was at least thirty minutes long. And since I could remember the details of that day well, even without reliving it, it could not grab my attention in the way the memories from twenty or more years ago did, and which I almost forgot.

When it began, I did not know that this was the last scene of my life review. But when it continued for thirty minutes, I suspected that I could not reach the next scene because there was not any. I understood that my life review was about to end and I became very excited.

I was curious to find out what kind of a place the afterlife would be and I really wanted to meet my grandmother, who was at that moment sitting in front of me and eating a piece of my birthday cake. I always missed her very much, but this feeling was never so strong as now, when I knew there was hardly any time left before the encounter. I really wanted to meet her!

And when this wish was formulated for the third or fourth time—like on command—the last scene of my life review ended.

Probably it could last longer, because it did not end as suddenly as it happened when Yin and Yang had dropped me out from the passageway. This time the picture darkened slowly, the sound weakened until it became silent, and finally blackness took over the place. Most likely, our creators made the life review to end when our wish to meet one of our deceased loved ones reached a certain point. It seemed like something or someone knew exactly when I was ready to move on.

The black silence did not last for long. I saw a light. First just a thin, blindingly white light beam appeared in the darkness—and yes, it really looked like that so many times mentioned tunnel—but soon the picture became clear. For a short time, everything was white as snow and then everything became pure slowly. After a while I could see crystal clear a very familiar place.

– 19 –

It was a beautiful spring morning when I arrived in the afterlife. However, a few hours earlier, my life had ended on a cloudy autumn afternoon in the hospital.

I was not surprised at all that my life after death began on a spring day: it was my favorite season and I liked mornings the best. Even though I suspected that the place would be built of my best memories, I was astonished by the precise details! Yin believed that I would reach an important place after the life review, most probably my family home. Well, this assumption seemed to be true, what is more, it was almost perfect.

The only difference was that I was not in my house but in front of it. Most precisely, I was standing in the street and I saw the outside of our home. It was like traveling back in time: the house looked exactly like in my childhood, even though it had changed a lot since then. It became nicer and bigger. I quickly realized that I saw my home in this way, because I was the happiest at that time. As I have been told before, the organ of the soul knows exactly which part of my life was attached to the nicest memories. So, anyone who decided what my first scene in the afterlife would look like, most probably wanted to make me happy. Only this could be the reason why my house appeared in the same way as it was in my childhood.

I was looking at the house from the dusty and muddy street and I could not decide what to do. I was standing motionless in the silence of the suburb: the birds were singing, but I could not see anybody. I felt like I was the only man in the world, or at least the only one in the neighborhood.

One of the reasons why I was motionless was that during my life review I could have watched everything from only one perspective. I could not look around even if I wanted to. Additionally, I had had to sit in one place for hours as Yin and Yang's subject for their experiment, even though I had a body then. Also, in the hospital I had been bedridden and forced to give up moving. But now, I was neither lying nor sitting but standing and waiting for something to happen.

I realized the fact that I was not a spectator anymore only when I tried to turn my head, and to my biggest surprise, I succeeded in it! If, for any reason, I might have thought that I was still watching my life review, at this point I would realize for sure that this was not a scene anymore but something different: an entirely new situation.

In a non-material world—where we do not have bodies—it is a huge change to be able to turn our heads. This new state is obviously not part of the life review, it is not anymore reliving a scene. It is something else...

Of course, I grabbed the opportunity and looked around carefully in the street. Each detail was in its right place, even the smallest particles of dust were copied perfectly from the world I remembered from my childhood. I automatically began comparing the old memories with the newer ones, which started by remembering the day I was at home for the last time. It was six months ago, and at that time our street had already been asphalted. The old dirt road's only privilege, the silence, was disrupted by cars from time to time.

And then something unbelievable happened! The dirt road became paved in a few seconds! And after a minute a car raced by! Everything happened as previously imagined. I could not believe my eyes! It was thousands or even millions of times more realistic than any kind of high-technology movie. It is not an exaggeration to say that it felt like reality.

I was so astonished by the view that I could not do anything for many long minutes. I was just staring at the road which became a paved street from a dusty, small dirt road in a very extraordinary way. There is and will never be such a visual effect that might resemble such a transformation! It is needless to say how shocked I was...

It took me some time to comprehend what had happened, and after that I needed to try this trick again. I wondered where the limits, if any, might be. What would happen if I imagined something unreal?

I did not want this question to remain unanswered, so I thought about the following: to make my street change into a river on which an unbelievably tall ship will sail across. I quickly stepped down from the road, I turned my back to the house and the heavenly miracle began within a few seconds.

As a first step, the road became water in a very amazing way. The asphalt crumbled and the dust turned into water. As if the asphalt road had broken down into its atoms in order to rearrange them later and to create a new material: water. Or better to say, only the picture of it. So, the river appeared in front of my house and when I bowed and turned my head to the left, I saw an unbelievably tall ship coming. Just as I had imagined before.

The river was not wider than an average street in a small town, since it had taken its place. It was so narrow that it was more like a canal. And a ship, that was at least a hundred meters tall and unrealistically narrow, was sailing towards me on that canal!

It did not take long for the ship to appear in front of the house. It was quiet, and what is more, its cutting through the water could not be heard either—probably because I had not imagined these sounds previously. Due to its unreal height it covered the sun that was lying low in the morning hours. Standing in the shadow of the ship, something occurred to me...

I thought it would be exciting to see the view from the top of the ship. I wondered how high I could jump in the afterlife where—as I have just realized—there were no physical boundaries. Thus, without much hesitation, I jumped!

While I was rising so quickly that I was almost flying, I was only thinking of having to reach the top. And I succeeded in it without any trouble. The stunt took ten seconds at most. I arrived to the top of this special ship which was only a few meters wide. If this had happened during my life, I might have fainted, or probably I would have been very scared. Most likely, I would have gone to the middle of the narrow place, where I would have sat or lied down in order to hold to something.

But now I was unbelievably brave, I was not afraid of anything, and of course, I did not feel dizziness. First, I looked at my home, and later I tried to find the houses of my friends—which was not easy from such height and in such enormous shadow. I also wanted to find the apartment complex where I had moved five years ago, but I could not. It seemed that I had created a ship that was way too tall. Anyway, Yin and Yang were perfectly right when they said that in the afterlife everything was possible!

After this, I jumped from the ship, but to be more precise, I just stepped down. I had to realize that the feeling was not like falling at all. I did not feel, for instance, that the wind cut my face. And I realized that I did not feel it while flying towards the top either. The falling also took around ten seconds and since the ship was moving all the time, I reached the ground a few houses further.

As I had imagined it, I landed on my feet. I was surprised a little that this enormous free fall did not have any physical consequences. Of course, I did not expect that it would be exactly like jumping from this height in the real world, but it was strange that I did not feel anything—either mentally or physically. So, I was disappointed in the afterlife a little bit...

I was walking towards my childhood home, when I remembered that it had been of different color for a long time, not white as presented. I knew what would happen in a moment, but still, I became astonished once again! The snow-white house became green in a second. Exactly as it looked like at the time of my death. I could not believe how beautiful and artistic the process of the transformation was.

When I reached the gate, I saw a strange mixture of my old and new memories and my adventure on the ship. The house was the same as in the time of my death, the fence and the gate looked like they did twenty years ago, and instead of the street a narrow river was flowing. I changed back the river into the street without any effort, but I did not bother with the fence and the gate.

Just like the most people, I was truly and obliviously happy during my childhood. However, my home's and the street's newer appearance was a more familiar and more homelike surrounding for me. According to the signs, the organ of the soul did not know this about me. It seems that this was not our creators' most important factor when they had decided which memories would be used for building up our first environment in the afterlife.

A minute later I also realized that the organ of the soul did not only keep record of the time when we were the happiest but also of who we would like to meet the most from those souls, who were already in the afterlife.

– 20 –

When I opened the gate and began walking, I was not sure whether there would be someone in the house. However, I knew if there was somebody, it could only be my grandmother.

It was not hard to guess: only my grandmother and I had died in the close family. And during my life review I also realized that it had ended when I wished to meet her so much. Probably, one of the aims of this screening was to find out who we would like to meet the most from our deceased loved ones. After all, it would be senseless to begin our existence at the afterlife, for example, in the company of a distant relative, with whom we did not have a close relationship even before death.

Anyway, I did not have much time to think about it, because I was standing in front of the door. I waited for a second, but I was so curious to find out whether there would be someone in the house that I opened the door without much hesitation. First, I realized that the interior was also the same as in my childhood memories. So, from the outside my home looked like on the day of my death, but from the inside it was exactly like approximately twenty years ago.

I could hear from the hall that someone was, most probably, cooking in the kitchen. I quickly opened the door between the hall and the kitchen. My grandmother turned and opened her eyes wide when she saw me.

"Grandmother!" I exclaimed and my eyes were filled with tears, which I did not realize at that moment, because I could not feel tears flowing on my cheek.

"Give me a hug!" she said and she cleared the tears from my face after a long hug.

She was also moved, but it turned out that she had a different reason for it. I saw on her face happiness, sadness and surprise at the same time. After her first question, I understood why:

"Why did *you* come?"

"Well, grandmother, I died very early," I said. "Six months ago I went to the doctor's because I felt pain in my..."

"Please, stop!" she interrupted me. It is true that she was smiling, but I felt that this was not that natural and comforting smile she always used to have. "I do not want to hear how you died. It is not important here..."

"All right," I said.

"Just tell me how many years you lived. I see you just the way you looked the last time we met..."

"Don't you feel how much time has passed since your death?"

"Not really," she answered uncertainly.

"Sadly, only a year has passed after your leaving. And believe me, it is very good that you see me in this way and not as I looked before my death," I said and I was glad she did not see me when I was skin and bone.

"All right, don't talk about it, it is unnecessary," she said and her smile was still not perfect, but it was more sincere than earlier.

"It hasn't appeared in your head how I looked on the day of my death, has it?" I asked with a rightful fear, because I could not keep any thought to myself on Yin and Yang's planet.

"What are you talking about?" she asked. "I do not understand you."

"All right, nothing, it is not important," I said feeling a relief.

"You are right, let's skip this topic. Give me a hug again!" she said, and finally, I did not see any signs of pain on her face. Luckily, she accepted quickly the fact of my early death and I was very happy about it, because I also thought it was not worth talking about it in the afterlife.

Once again we hugged each other for a long time, but now I realized even more that it did not feel the same as when we were alive.

"Did you also notice..." I began my question, but I could not finish it because of my grandmother's immediate answer. She knew exactly what I was talking about. After all, she had been here for a longer period of time.

"Here the things are just seemingly like in the real life," she said.

"Yes, I realized it even outside when I was in front of the house. But still, I find it strange that I do not feel your hug."

"Oh, darling," my grandmother said with an undoubtedly sincere smile. "There are even more interesting things here! Look!" and she pointed towards the stove where French toasts and spinach were being prepared. "Isn't it strange as well?"

"What exactly?" I asked.

"Well, that you cannot smell anything."

"Now, that you have mentioned..." I was surprised, and not because of the fact that there were no odors in the afterlife but because I did not notice the lack of smell associated with cooking until my grandmother had mentioned it.

"You know that I always put a lot of garlic in the spinach," she continued. "And now, I grated almost a whole clove of garlic, but you cannot smell it. Not even on my fingers. This is stranger than not feeling each other's hug, right?"

"Yes, you are right," I agreed and I remembered that my grandmother must have been surprised very much when she had arrived here. She, unlike me, has not been given any kind of preparation for this form of existence. I began thinking whether I should talk her about the experiment, but I decided that it was too early for that.

At the same time, my grandmother saw on my face that my surprise did not last for a long time. Because of it she might feel that it was high time she unveiled some additional details:

"Do you see the lunch?" she turned towards the stove where the lunch was being prepared.

"Of course," I answered with a smile on my face.

"Now, turn and look at the table!"

I did as she said and the lunch was there, served tastefully. When I looked back to the stove, it was empty.

"What do you think about this?" she asked with a proud smile.

"This is unbelievable!" I answered, probably too theatrically.

I pretended to be astonished, because I was afraid my grandmother would feel uncomfortable if I told her that I had already created a hundred-meter tall and two or three-meter wide ship, from which I had even jumped off, just a few minutes after my arrival in the afterlife. I believed I had an enormous privilege, but I did not want to take advantage of it. So, I promised myself once again that I would not tell her where I had spent some time after my death and before the afterlife.

But life often changes people's plans and—as it turned out later—this could happen in the afterlife as well...

All in all, my grandmother believed that this time she had succeeded in amusing me with her trick. This made me feel both happy and guilty. I could not stop thinking that I got to this awkward situation only because I had heard from Yin and Yang an almost perfect theory about the afterlife. If only I had not dropped into that experiment! How much more effective would my grandmother's show have been...

While I was thinking about it, my grandmother probably thought I was trying to guess how she had managed to do such things. And this made me feel even guiltier. But happily, my grandmother broke the silence:

"Do you want to know how I did that?" she asked while still having that proud smile on her face.

"Of course!" I lied to her.

"Curiosity killed the cat!" she said with her forefinger pointing at me. For a moment her face turned serious. And then she added almost laughing: "First things first!"

"All right," I said with a smile on my face. I believed that she probably wanted to tell me the information slowly, step by step. I understood her entirely, because I would have done it in the same way.

To continue the show, my grandmother snapped her fingers and the dishes disappeared from the table. Then she opened the cupboard in order to show that they had reached their place. Of course, being clean.

"As you can see," she began the explanation, "if you do not want to do something or wait for it, you do not need to."

"How interesting..." I said.

"But I must tell you that I did this only because of you. Usually, I do everything myself, because I like it more when the things resemble real life as much as possible here."

"What do you mean?" I asked.

"Well, I always finish cooking and then I set the table. I also wash the dishes and put them into the cupboard. Oh! I had not asked whether you were hungry, because I had known you were not. And I have bad news: you will never be here!" she added laughing.

"But what do you do with the meals you have cooked?" I asked, and I really became curious because I did not know the answer.

"I make them disappear."

"Like you did a few minutes ago?"

"Yes. But I leave some scraps of food on the plate to create an impression I had been eating. The dish washing is more realistic in this way."

"So, we cannot eat here?" I asked.

"Actually, we can..." she answered and she stepped to the refrigerator. "Open and look inside."

I did as she told me. The fridge was empty.

"And now, listen!" she closed the door of the fridge and her next trick began. "A huge chocolate cake!" she said and asked me to look into the fridge again. When I opened the door, the cake was there.

"Well, this is really amazing!" I said and I closed the door.

"Pizza!" she said the next spell and an enormous pizza appeared in the fridge.

"Well, grandma, I am so sorry we could not do such things while we were alive!" I said with a smile. This is how I tried to resolve the tension I felt due to the fact that I was only pretending to be surprised.

"There is only one catch..."

"What is it?" I asked.

"Nothing has a taste!" she said with a sad smile. "The food neither smells nor tastes. And when you swallow something, you do not feel anything. You can eat whatever amount, you will feel neither the taste of the meal nor fullness."

Then I felt sorry for my grandmother, because she had always liked eating. She must have been very disappointed when she had realized there were no gastronomic pleasures in the afterlife. But she did not let me feel sad for long, because she made a joke out of it:

"I am so sorry that my doctor ordered me to be on a diet in my last years of life!"

"Well, yes..." I began after a good laugh. "Even if we cannot eat, we can at least laugh heartily here!" I replied with another joke.

"And this trick does not work with food only. Look! Money!" she said and opened the fridge which was full of money.

"It is also useless here, right?"

"Of course," she nodded. "But come, I will show you the house. You have already seen the kitchen. Let me show you the bathroom!"

"It used to look like this a long time ago..." I thought when we entered.

"If there is anything entirely unnecessary here, than it is this!" she said partly smiling, partly seriously. "We never use the toilet, we do not need to brush our teeth, to take a bath or to dry our hair... The bathroom is totally useless."

I was just looking and listening to my grandmother, who continued her seemingly sincere complaints:

"At least, I can do something in the kitchen: I can act as if I was cooking or baking, even though the food has neither taste nor smell, only the looks. But the bathroom is very disappointing. Once, I laid in the bathtub to take a hot bath, because I had always enjoyed it. But I did not feel anything!"

I did not know how to react. I realized that she did not really like the bathroom, so I offered to go to the living room.

"I spend more time here," she said. "Because of television."

"Can we watch TV here?" I asked, and finally, there was something that intrigued me.

"Well, so-so."

"What do you mean?"

"I can only watch something that I had already seen at least once throughout my life. I sit down on the couch and I do not even need to turn on the TV. It is enough to imagine my favorite series' beginning and it begins immediately. But I can watch only the older episodes. I can also watch just older news."

"Yes, this is logical," I thought to myself.

"On the day when I died," my grandmother continued, "there was supposed to be a very exciting episode of my favorite series, but I could not watch it. You cannot imagine how happy I was when I reached this place and I saw that there was a television, and in addition it was working! But my disappointment was even bigger when I understood that the new episodes were not available..."

"However, it is still better than nothing, right?" I asked.

"Well, yes, of course. You can also watch your favorite movies or you can reread your favorite books. The ones you have seen or read already can be found here."

Then I looked at the bookcase and I saw a snow-white, almost luminous book. It was not familiar to me at all, either from my childhood or adulthood. I stepped there and grabbed it to take a look at it.

"Oh, well..." my grandmother began. She sighed and became very serious. "I wanted to talk about this later, after you have spent already some time here, but if you have seen it..."

So, I took the book and if there was air in the afterlife, it would have been a breathtaking moment! I could not believe my eyes when I saw the title of the book: *The Meaning of Life.*

"What kind of book is this?" I asked excitedly.

"This is a special one. It can be found in each house here. This is the only thing in the afterlife that could not be changed or made to disappear. And its content is new for everyone."

"And what is it about?"

"Well, it says what the aim of our existence is. Not of this life but the real one."

"This is unbelievable!" I was shocked.

But my grandmother was looking at me with such an expressionless face as she was not interested at all.

"You don't need to take it seriously," she said. "The one who wrote it had no idea what life was like. In their opinion life can be only nice, and what is more, it consists of pleasure only... Such nonsense!"

"I cannot believe this..." I thought.

"At the beginning of the book it is stated," my grandmother continued, "that every new-comer has to read it. But if you ask me, it is entirely in vain, because there is not a single word which is true in it."

"I agree, it is unnecessary to read it," I said when my shock was gone. "But only because I know exactly what it is about."

"Don't be silly! It is stated that we can read this book only after death. So it is sure that you do not know what it is about. I cannot say that it is not an interesting book, but life is not at all like it is pictured in it..."

"But I know exactly what this book is about and you will not believe how!"

– 21 –

"I do not know where to begin..." I said after a few seconds, when I saw that my grandmother understood I was not joking.

"But how can you possibly know what the book is about?" she asked seriously.

"OK, I can prove it, it is not a problem," I said and I sat down on the couch after putting down the almost blindingly white book on the table. "Probably, it is stated in the book that we were born in order to enjoy life at its most, in other words: to enjoy every pleasure of the material world. We have not only been given a body but also intellectual abilities that are unique among all the living beings. We can experience physical pleasures like eating fine food or having sex, and we can also enjoy the process of artistic creation and art pieces made by others, such as books, pictures and music. Did I guess it right?" I asked with a smile on my face.

"Yes, you did..." my grandmother said, and she could not even hide her shock. "But how do you know this? The book states that we are all born ignorant of this information. And we will not recognize it during our lifetime. We will know what the aim of our existence is only after our death. This is how the system works. Because if we knew what the meaning of our life is..."

"...we would not enjoy it so much," I ended her sentence.

"But how do you know this?" she repeated her previous question.

"How should I begin... Is there in the book something about other planets where people live just like on the Earth?"

"No, not at all."

"Well, it is not surprising," I thought to myself. "Our creators believed that it did not matter which planet we were born on because, in theory, the same life awaited us everywhere."

"Why is it important whether there are people on other planets?" my grandmother asked.

"Well, the truth is that half an hour ago I was on another planet, not on the Earth."

"What are you talking about?"

"However, I died on the Earth. At least, for the first time."

"I do not understand you..."

"After my death something strange happened, while I was watching my life review," I began my story.

"Was maybe everything explained to you about the meaning of life and the world during your life review? Is this why you know everything?"

"No, no. Something completely different happened. My life review was interrupted after approximately an hour and I woke up on another planet in another body."

My grandmother remained speechless, so I continued:

"There are plenty of planets where people live. On one of them the inhabitants have become so developed in science that they can connect to the passageway through which the souls travel after death to the afterlife. They cannot choose which soul to catch, and accidentally I was one of the stopped ones..."

"This is unbelievable..."

"Yes, it was strange for me as well. I spent there only a few hours, but during this time I learned everything about the life and the world. I mean, everything that those very smart people have discovered so far. And I can see only now how smart they are, because they have found out the content of this book by themselves," I pointed to *The Meaning of Life*. "They have deduced the answers during their lifetime. They did not have to die in order to know what this book is about. So, grandma, they were the ones who had informed me. This is why I know everything."

"But life is not at all like it is presented in this book..."

"Great you have mentioned it! I have almost forgotten the main point!" I said a little absent-mindedly. "It seems that the Earth is an exception. Life is not as it should be only on our planet. Only we have diseases, wars, hatred, poverty and everything bad which you cannot find in this book for sure, because originally such things were not meant for us."

"Are you serious?"

"Yes, I am. On every other planet people enjoy their lives in peace and health. Exactly like it is written in this book."

"I cannot believe it..."

"So, grandma, I understand your feelings about this book. I would also think it is pointless, if I had reached directly this place after my death..."

"Do you know what is interesting?" she disrupted me.

"What?"

"While I was reading this book, my first thought was that maybe once, in the distant past, life on the Earth looked like this. But we ruined something, and this is why today we do not live like we should, like it is written in this book."

"It was not us who made a mistake," I said. "But our creators."

"Our creators?"

"Yes, those who had created all this. I am sure that they wrote this book as well."

"Unbelievable..."

"Sadly, our creators did not think about some possible consequences..."

"What do you mean?"

"Their biggest mistake about the Earth was that a disproportionate amount of comets reached our planet."

"Sorry?"

"The book does not say how they spread the life seeds?" I asked.

"No..."

"It seems they did not give out every secret of theirs," I thought.

"Is it important?"

"Yes, it is very important. The point is that the first living beings, which were simple but very tough and almost indestructible microorganisms, were sent in huge blocks of ice to the Universe by an enormous explosion."

"The Big Bang..." she added.

"Yes," I nodded and I was very surprised that my

grandmother was familiar with this concept. “So, too many comets landed on the Earth resulting in a planet full of water and life seeds. In this way the conditions were more than ideal to begin the evolutionary process.”

“But I still do not understand what the problem was.”

“According to the original plan, only one evolution should take place on one planet. And in the end, only one human species should appear. However, on the Earth the conditions were so good that more evolutionary processes started, but of course, not exactly at the same time. The comets were continuously arriving, and in the end more human species with different levels of development appeared on the same planet.”

“I see,” my grandmother said. “It is like someone had collected people with various levels of development from different planets, and then put them all down on the Earth.”

“Yes, this is a very good analogy!” I said and I had to realize again that my grandmother was surprisingly wise. She seemed much smarter than she used to be in her life...

“So, did this cause animosity?” she asked.

“Exactly,” I answered. “Animosity, hatred, our nature to divide people to groups and to believe that our group is better and more valuable than others, has such ancient roots. This all is the consequence of the ancient blending.”

"The ancient blending?"

"That is the name we gave to this phenomenon. Obviously, the ancient human species reproduced among each other. There is nothing strange about that, because they were all human beings. They were just not on the same level of development."

"And are the diseases also the consequence of the ancient blending?"

"No, something else caused them. But if you have mentioned the other consequences, I have to add that the ancient blending caused the diversity of people's knowledge and appearance. According to the original plan, we should be almost the same regarding our physical and mental characteristics!"

"It is very interesting. This cannot be found in the book."

"Our creators probably believed it was unnecessary to note down what everyone could realize throughout their lives. As I have said, this is the case on each planet, except the Earth. Only our species is blended, which means that the baby born on our planet can have whatever amount of the characteristics of the differently developed human species that blended in the past. And this also refers to the number of the cells of the organ of the soul."

"Well, this is mentioned in the book. I read that we were deliberately set to a lower intellectual level by means of the organ of the soul. This also opens the passageway towards the afterlife," my grandmother said.

"This is true," I said and I could not stop wondering how informed my grandmother had become. "The organ of the soul is an amazing masterpiece of our creators," I continued. "And during the design of it they made their other big mistake."

"Is the problem that they made us to be less intelligent until we were alive?"

"No, the fact is that they did not succeed in it. This is the problem!"

"What do you mean?"

"It does not surprise me that you did not read about this in the book. Our creators had not suspected this to happen. They forgot that the soul cells would also divide as any other cell in our body. At every birth their quantity doubles and this is why every generation is smarter than the previous one."

"So, this is why science develops," my grandmother concluded.

"Yes." I approved. "By the passage of time we will become so enlightened that we will discover our creators' every secret. And when it happens, we cannot enjoy the material existence anymore. Curiosity, or in other words: science, should have never appeared according to the original plan. On every other planet this is the only mistake, and it caused a big problem, but on the Earth, strangely, it has advantages as well. For instance, science fights diseases and in this way helps people in having a better life..."

"...but sadly, it also helps in making wars much efficient," my grandmother added.

"You could not say it more nicely."

"So, what is the cause of the diseases?" she asked curiously.

"On our planet evolution was stopped and restarted many times. After every mass extinction most of the complex living beings disappeared, however, the tough microorganisms always survived, thus, they had much time to strengthen. They had a great advantage regarding those living beings which appeared later. The reason why there are no diseases on other planets is that there was only one evolution on them, and it was not disrupted but happened as our creators had imagined."

"I see," my grandmother said.

"As we had realized a few hours ago on the other planet," I continued, "the Earth was very near to the place from where the life seeds had been sent. This is the cause of all the mistakes that appeared on our planet only. The comets came more often and the impact period lasted much longer than on any other planet. This led to the enormous quantity of water, to more evolutionary processes and to catastrophes that caused a lot of mass extinctions."

"Well, I am glad to hear these things, because now I

know that someone else is the cause of the many maleficent things on the Earth, not we."

"I agree," I said. "But if you think about it, it is very unfair to have such lives. Of course, there are people who had relatively nice lives on the Earth, but most do not have an easy life."

Seemingly, my grandmother became sad.

"Why are you so sad?" I asked.

"Because of you. I was lucky to live seventy-nine years. I did have some diseases, but none of them was severe. But you lost your life at such a young age..."

"Oh, grandma, isn't it you who has told me a few minutes ago that this topic is not important here? That it is unnecessary to talk about it?"

"Yes, this is true, but still, it saddens me..."

"All right, never mind," I said and I turned to the table to pick up at the book once again. "Well," I continued with a smile, "you were right when you said it was completely useless to read this book."

"What to say... I was very surprised that you knew exactly what it was about."

"And still, this is not the biggest punch of all!"

"Why? What is it?"

"We, the inhabitants of the Earth, have read this book

in our lifetime! It can be found in almost every house on the bookcase."

"Sorry?"

"All right, not this book exactly," I said and I put back *The Meaning of Life* on the table. "But the Bible! Everything can be found in it!"

"In the Bible?" my grandmother asked confusedly.

"Yes. We agreed with the two scientists from the other planet that once in the past a traveling civilization had visited the Earth. Probably, they were people whose planet had become uninhabitable, so they were trying to find a new home while traveling by spaceships. They were communicating by means of telepathy with the people who lived on the Earth then. However, we did not understand them perfectly, because they were more developed. That is why the stories in the Bible can be hardly interpreted."

"Oh my..."

"The story of Adam and Eve," I continued, "actually tells that after we had been created, our only task was to enjoy life and to avoid science. These concepts in the people's head appeared as the Garden of Eden and the tree of knowledge but still, the story can be easily understood. At least now, after I have also met members of a more developed civilization."

"I am at a loss what to say..."

"Even the story of evolution can be found in the Bible, since our holy book also claims that the living beings appeared in a certain order. So, the point is that the Bible is not a book full of invented stories, but at the same time it is not true that our creators were the ones who had contacted us."

"It was just a traveling civilization," my grandmother added.

"Yes, this is more than likely."

"And did these people stay on the Earth? After all, they had eventually found themselves a new planet to live on, so..."

"You see… We have never thought of it, but now that you have mentioned… There is a great possibility that they settled down on our planet."

"And they also blended with us, right?"

"Now this certainly has not occurred to us at all!" I said. "However, it also explains everything. If that civilization from the space decided to stay on the Earth, then that was the supposed very developed species with which we blended in the past. And if this is the case, then it was they who built the pyramids for example! But sadly, after blending with the people from the Earth, their knowledge disappeared. You must be right, grandma, this is a very good theory. But now, I have to ask you something."

"Yes?"

"I do not know how to begin. I do not want to hurt you, so I ask your forgiveness in advance. I noticed how smart you are. You are different than you used to be during my entire lifetime."

"No problem," she said with a smile on her face. "You did not hurt me, because you are right. It is time I told you something important. In the beginning, before you noticed the book, I had talked with you in a different way. I can even say that I pretended to be sillier," she laughed. "I was afraid that you would not understand everything, so I wanted to communicate the information slowly."

"I knew it!" I said. "And I did the same thing with you!" I added with a relief.

"Then this was a very strange situation, because you could not know that I became smarter here and I could not know that you arrived here enlightened. We both pretended to be dull in vain."

"So, you learned everything from this book?" I asked and I looked at *The Meaning of Life*.

"Of course not... I could hardly learn anything from it! And I could not do anything with the information I found in it. But now everything is clear, because I know that the Earth is just an exception where something went terribly wrong."

"But then, how did it happen that you are so smart and so informed?"

"Well..." my grandmother sighed, "the afterlife is a place where people become smart. Whether they like it or not."

"What do you mean?"

"You will see by the passage of time that the only real thing here is our communication. Everything else is just illusion. We cannot have real lives here. The only thing that resembles it, and which makes us happy, is the communication with each other. And those who do nothing else but share information among each other, become very smart after a certain time."

"A very logical consequence," I thought to myself.

"Of course, this also happens," my grandmother continued, "because nothing can be forgotten here. Our memory is unbelievably perfect. You cannot imagine the enormous quantity of knowledge that has been accumulated here. If you hear something once, you will automatically remember it. We simply cannot forget anything, because here we do not have brains which have a finite capacity."

"I see," I said.

"You meet a smart person, you have a talk with him and everything that was previously mentioned sticks to you. If you talk for a long time, you can even get his entire knowledge. And nobody is in a hurry here. You can especially learn a lot if you meet someone who has encountered many people before you. After collecting much information and meeting just enough people, you will become a smart and a well-informed person."

"Well, at least we can have a good chat and we can learn a lot here," I said.

"Yes, it is true. But believe me, the more time you spend here, the more you feel that you do not want to learn but to live..."

"Oh, grandma, don't tell me that you think that the afterlife is a bad place..."

She was just listening. To my biggest surprise she did not answer anything, so I had to ask the question again:

"You want to say that this is not a good place?"

"Well…" she sighed. "Would you like me to talk sincerely about the afterlife?"

"Of course I would!"

– 22 –

"As you have already seen, there are no culinary pleasures here," my grandmother began. "And believe me, even I could accept this easily. It also does not bother me that we are not able to breathe, because we were not constantly aware of this fact even when we were alive. The first major shock was that we could not sleep either."

"But we do not have bodies, so it is not surprising that we cannot sleep," I added.

"This is true, but in the first instance, I do not miss sleeping as a physical activity. Of course, I have felt many times that it would be so good to lay down in a comfortable bed, put my head onto a soft and fragrant pillow, feel the pleasant warmth of the blanket and have a nice sleep. Once I had tried, but it made me very sad. It was highly disappointing that I did not feel anything of the above mentioned..."

"But why is it a problem for you that we cannot sleep here?"

"I would like to "switch off" sometimes. I miss that

feeling very much."

"Just because we got used to it on the Earth?"

"Well, maybe. But in my opinion, it is about something else. You do not miss sleeping yet, because you are a new one here. But after a certain time you will also wish to have a good sleep. I cannot explain why: neither physical nor mental tiredness exist here, but after some time you will feel that it is high time you went to sleep. To "switch off" somehow after such a long and continuous wakefulness."

"The reason could be that there are no real days and nights here. Don't you think so?"

"No. It has nothing to do with that. There are days and nights here whenever and as long as we want. And in order to say something positive about the afterlife: it is a small consolation but you can create here beautiful sunsets and moonlit nights."

"I can imagine it..."

"So, everything is nice and good, but if I compare the two, I have to say that the absence of sleep takes away from this place much more than the ability to create any kind of environment adds to it."

"But this is not the biggest problem, is it?"

"You guess it right," my grandmother said and nodded. "However, if you asked me to name concretely what is the biggest problem, I could not choose only one thing. But everything I dislike here has one thing in common: the things are not independent from us."

"What do you mean?"

"You will understand it best if I tell you what the first—and at the same time the last—card game with my friend, Eve was like. You must remember her. She used to live at the corner before moving to her son due to her illness."

"Of course I remember her," I said.

"We decided to play rummy. We sat in the kitchen, I offered her orange juice and I had even baked biscuits. As I have already told you, I like if this kind of life resembles the true one, at least in its appearance... So, I was the one who shuffled and dealt the cards and I can even say that, despite the tasteless biscuits and orange juice, we enjoyed the game at first. But then, Eve put down her cards with a broad smile. And this ended our good mood."

"Why, what happened next?" I asked and curiosity could be heard in my voice.

"I was very surprised what I saw. Eve had all the jokers and it was a huge problem, because I also had them all!" my grandmother laughed. "When I showed her my jokers, we looked at each other and realized immediately that it was senseless to continue the game. Unlike in the real life, here everyone gets the cards they want. It is enough to think about all the jokers and you will get them."

"I see..." I said. "Such games cannot be enjoyable..."

"Not at all. But what can one expect when the cards are not real either..."

"So, for example, if we played the lottery, we would all win the jackpot, right?"

"Exactly," my grandmother answered. "But why would we play the lottery when money does not have any value here? And anyway, we can create whatever amount of money whenever we want it."

"This is true..."

"The television is another good example that nothing is independent from us," she continued. "In the beginning, I just told you that I could watch only those episodes of my favorite series, which I had already seen once in my life. Of course, it is not a lie, but then I did not want to confuse you, I did not want to give too much information. This is why I did not tell you that when I had arrived here and watched TV for the first time, my series continued exactly where it had stopped before my death."

"Really?" I asked in surprise.

"Wait and see!" my grandmother said smiling. "The series really continued, but I was the one who directed it!"

"You?"

"Yes, with my thoughts. At first, I did not realize that

everything happened to the actors according to my wish, but it turned out very quickly that even the series was not independent from me. And from that point on, it was not interesting at all, because I knew exactly that I would see on TV what I had previously imagined. It is not the same..."

"Yes, I see."

"I would like so much to watch an episode of my favorite series that would surprise me! Which was directed by someone else, and where I would not know what would happen next. I really miss the feeling of amazement..."

"But when I entered the kitchen, it seemed that you were surprised."

"Yes, because I was not expecting you."

"I know... But according to this, amazement *can* take place here."

"It really can, but only another person, another soul can cause it. As I have said, the only real thing here is our communication, which means that, fortunately, I never know in advance what you will tell me. However, the time will come when you will have told me everything, and after that we will not know what to talk about. But let's not hurry, afterlife will still be a bearable place for you in the next few hours..."

"Grandmother, this sounds very disappointing."

"You wanted me to be honest."

"This is true..."

"Here," she continued, "the nicest moments are those when one of your loved ones arrive. Everyone looks forward to it very much. After so many unnecessarily prepared lunches, games played without excitement and films without any unexpected turns someone suddenly appears with whom you can talk for long. The newcomers are very happy to see you again, and you can hear the things that happened after your death to your family. Finally, something new happens, you can hear new things. Such meetings are very rare and appreciated moments here. But sooner or later, there will be no more topics, no more experiences which you can recall, and sadly, the period of eternal silence will begin, when there is nothing to say to each other anymore. Of course, if we could gain new experiences, life could be much better here. However, this is impossible."

"Why?" I asked.

"Well, is it an experience if everyone gets the best cards at each game?"

"No..." I admitted.

"And this is true for everything else here. If you go fishing, you will get as many and as big fishes as you would like to. If you go to a city where you have never been before, you will see it exactly like you have previously imagined it. I am sure that you understand what I am talking about, so there is no point in listing more examples."

"Yes, I see," I said calmly. "So, afterlife is such a place..."

"Well, yes..."

"But when I arrived here, I created a river from the street and I even made a huge ship. Its shadow was so big that it reached the school. I jumped to the ship, and later I jumped off!"

"Oh, I have already been to the Moon," my grandmother said with a smile.

"Really?"

"Yes. I traveled by a very long escalator. It began in the backyard, and ran all the way to the Moon."

"It must have been interesting!" I said.

"Well, it was, but only for the first time..."

"What do you mean?"

"Such adventures are only interesting until you repeat them. How did you feel, for example, when you jumped off that ship?"

"Well, of course, not exactly the same as I would in my real life..."

"What was the difference?"

"During the free fall the wind did not cut my face, my

shirt did not flutter..."

"...and you suspected that when you landed, nothing bad could happen," my grandmother added.

"Yes, this is true."

"You see, this is what I was talking about. If you do it again, you will know exactly what is going to happen with you, thus, there will be no excitement at all. Believe me, it will not be interesting."

"I believe you."

"Anyway, the book explains this nicely," my grandmother continued, and she looked at *The Meaning of Life*. "It says that the material world is the perfect opposite of the afterlife. Here we are immortal, extremely smart and we cannot enjoy the pleasures of the material existence, however, our real lives are finite but at least they are full of joy. What is more, they consist of nothing but pleasure. Except on the Earth, of course," she added quickly. "Regarding the remarkable intelligence, we are designed to be less smart while we are alive, but in my opinion, it is not a problem."

"I agree," I said. "Now I see that our creators wanted to protect us from having such a boring, uneventful and unexciting life in the material world, just like we have here in the afterlife. It was very disappointing what I saw on that other planet. They are so smart that their lives are already almost exactly like this one. However, according to the original plan, only the afterlife should be so uneventful."

"How ironic..." my grandmother added. "On the Earth just the opposite is true. We believe that our life, which is very often hardly enjoyable and difficult, will be followed by a beautiful one in the afterlife..."

"Yes," I said. "This is very ironic and sad. But if I think about all those horrible things, it is not surprising that the people on the Earth imagine the afterlife as a good place. Many of them have so bad lives that when their troubles had ended and they reached here, even this boring place would seem like heaven. What to say, I would not go back to my hospital bed to continue suffering either... So, this really is heaven, at least in the sense that there are no diseases here, we cannot starve and we are not stressed because of financial problems..."

"Here is the biggest possible equality between us..." my grandmother added.

"This is true," I agreed. "And of course, there are no wars, no violent deaths: the one who does not have a body cannot be murdered either."

"What is more, no crime can happen here," she added.

"Well, yes... From this point of view it is not a bad place at all. And do you know what is also ironic?"

"What?"

"Due to the so many bad things on the Earth, we believe that not only one but two afterlives exist. We hope that there is a heaven and a hell, separate places for good and bad people. We think that many people did not get the deserved punishment during their life, so we believe that they will get it at least in the afterlife. And how disappointed the people on the Earth would be, if they knew that the theory about two afterlives was entirely nonsense. Because, according to the original plan, every person should be very similar, i.e. it must not even occur to us to take away other's property, hurt people or to kill them. Everyone should live in peace and harmony so, as a result, crime would not exist. But how could the people on the Earth know such things..."

My grandmother was silent. Even though it seemed she would like to say something, I had to finish my thought:

"However, the two scientists I met on the other planet imagined the afterlife very good, we can say even perfect. It did not even occur to them that there might be two afterlives. And also, one of their biggest fears was that this place was boring and uneventful. As I see, they imagined it very well."

"But they are not right..." my grandmother said.

"OK..." I began. "I have to admit that I was exaggerating a little. The afterlife is not entirely an uneventful place..."

"No, no," my grandmother interrupted me. "I was thinking about the other thing you said."

"Which one?"

"They are not right that only one afterlife exists."

"Sorry?" I asked in astonishment.

"I understand that the people you met did not need to suspect that bad people would be treated differently in the afterlife, because there are no bad people on their planet. But one thing is sure: no one has ever met a person here who killed another man or made his life harder in any way. It cannot be a coincidence that all the bad people are missing."

"Is this why grandfather is not in the house?"

"I think so," my grandmother answered.

"I believed that you did not want to be with him. I know that he was an alcoholic and that he treated you badly, and my mum also when she was a child. I did not want to mention it at all."

"I understand you."

"So, is he now in hell?"

"I cannot be one hundred percent sure about this, but in my opinion, he is there."

"And cannot it happen that he also reached this place like you and me, but he had already gone away?"

"What do you mean?"

"Well, for example, that he had been reborn before your arrival. He died almost thirty years before you, so..."

"No, no," my grandmother stopped me. "He cannot be reborn, and this is something that I am one hundred percent sure about. It is stated in the book."

"So, we can have only one life..." I said and I remembered that this was the answer that Yin and Yang had been desperately searching for.

"No, we can have several ones," my grandmother said. "We can go back living whenever we want to. At least in theory."

"Sorry?" I asked in a confused way.

"The book tells us how we can be reborn, and theoretically, we can do it countless times. But for some reason it does not work. Our creators stopped the whole system, but thanks to you, now I understand why!"

"And why?" I asked and I was very happy, because I knew that, at least for a while, the afterlife would not be such a boring place for me, as it was previously described by my grandmother.

– 23 –

"In my opinion," my grandmother began, "they stopped the process of rebirth, because they had realized that there was a planet where something went terribly wrong. Where the people, beyond their control, do not live such lives as our creators intended them."

"Is this how they try to protect the people from birth on the Earth?"

"I think so. Only in this way it makes sense that they stopped the system. Until you came, we had not had the clue that people lived on other planets as well, and that life was full of beauty and pleasure everywhere except on the Earth. So, I used to believe that they had temporarily stopped the process of rebirth to prevent bad people from escaping, i.e. from getting a new life."

"But this is also a logical theory," I said.

"It is, but it is illogical that we, who are not in hell, cannot be reborn either."

"Have you tried it?" I asked the question, a little bit disappointed.

"Of course not! It did not even occur to me, because I wanted to meet you in the first place. However, my friend Eve and others tried it several times, but without any success. And they do not understand why they, who have never caused any harm to anybody, cannot go back to the Earth hoping for a better new life."

"And what is the process of rebirth?" I asked with curiosity.

"It is very simple. You just need to cover your eyes with the book," she pointed to *The Meaning of Life*.

"Is that all?"

"Yes. As I have said, this book is very special: we cannot do anything to it, unlike to the other objects here. We cannot transform it or make it disappear, we cannot even tear a page from it. However, this is the only thing which can cause real darkness. For example, if you put any other object or your hand in front of your eyes, it will not make real darkness, because it is enough to think that you can see through it, and it will become transparent immediately."

"This really is the case," I said after I had tried out the trick using my right hand.

"The book says that if you want to be reborn, you have to lay down, open the book and put it on your face. After a few seconds you will disappear from this place, and without any memories you will begin your next life as a very small child. At least, in theory..."

"You are right that rebirth is simple in theory," I said. "And it is very probable that it does not work now because of the Earth. This might be some kind of precautionary measure, since the chances are unbelievably big that a soul will be born on the Earth."

"But there are many other planets, right?"

"Of course, but the problem is that on any other planet there are not as many inhabitants as in just one big city on the Earth. It can be possible that the Earth has a bigger population than all of the planets together in the Universe."

"Is this really possible?"

"In my opinion, yes. On the planet where I was a few hours ago, it turned out that the Earth was special because of its population as well. I have heard that on other planets there are only a few million people, but on the Earth there are more than seven billion of them. And this is not the final number, because the population grows at a very great speed…"

"You are right," my grandmother sighed. "Our creators must see the Earth as a tumor that is growing rapidly..."

"It might be the case," I agreed.

"Knowing this information, it was really a smart decision to stop the system. Otherwise, anyone who does not originate from the Earth, and would like to live in a body once again, would play Russian roulette. Those people do not even suspect how risky it would be if the process of rebirth worked. Now they just see that they cannot be reborn, but they do not understand why this is so. The people from the other planets had an incomparably better life than we had, thus, they must be waiting very much to leave this uneventful and boring environment in order to begin their second lives."

"Was this our first life?" I asked.

"Yes," my grandmother answered. "And before you ask me how I know it, I will tell you that I found this in the book. The information is reliable. We know how many lives we had based on the number of shortened lives we see after our death."

"In our life review, right?"

"Yes. After we died, we see a small reminder of each life's best moments. In the afterlife we remember our previous lives, but when we get a body, we forget everything."

"So, is this the main function of the life review?"

"Yes, it is. It shows how many lives we have had so far. And because I have never heard that anyone lived more times, or that someone met a soul that had such experience, I believe that everyone has had only one life so far."

"Isn't it possible that there are people who were born more times? Who had gone back to live again before our creators stopped the system? They obviously did not stop the process of rebirth immediately. If they had done so, we could not have gotten our first body."

"Yes, it might happen that such souls exist, but for example, I am sure that your grandfather is not one of them."

"How do you know?"

"I am sure that our creators did not hear for the first time that something went terribly wrong on one of the planets—just a few years ago. Before your grandfather there were hundreds of generations who could inform our creators that life was not enjoyable on the Earth..."

"But how could our creators hear anything from anyone? For instance, after my death I was never asked whether I was satisfied with my life or not..."

"Neither was I," my grandmother replied. "But they get the information somehow. It is obvious that the bad people are separated due to their deeds."

"This is a logical assumption," I added. "I began to believe that the whole system was set automatically and that our creators left us alone, thinking that everything went according to the original plan and that everything was all right."

"Well, it might be true that originally they imagined the system working in this way, but now it is obvious that it is not the case. They have turned off the process of rebirth, for example."

“You are right,” I said. “This is a strong argument that they are working on something at the moment.”

“So, if there was anyone on the Earth who was reborn, that person must have lived thousands of years ago.”

“And if he was lucky, he was not born on the Earth again,” I added.

“Yes...” my grandmother sighed, and it seemed that she began thinking about something carefully.

“What is on your mind, grandma?” I asked.

“I was thinking from where the souls come now into the newborn people if no one can be reborn?”

“Well...” I said. “This is a good question. Does this mean that the process of rebirth works? At least, for some souls?”

“I do not think so,” my grandmother answered. “Maybe everybody automatically gets the first life, and there are still many souls waiting for their turns.”

“Yes, this can be the case...” I said and we were silent for two or three seconds.

I was afraid that the eternal silence had begun already, but fortunately, I was frightened in vain. However, it was a bad sign that my grandmother was thinking about the same. She broke the silence with the following words:

"You know... If you had not visited that other planet, most probably we would not be talking now. Maybe, we would have run out of topics so far..."

"And what will happen when we really have nothing to talk about?" I asked. "What will we be doing then? Looking at each other in silence?"

"No, it does not make any sense. Until you go and find other people who are also here, I will stay in the house in order to wait for my daughters and their families and a few friends of mine."

"Won't you be bored?"

"I will be cooking in the kitchen, so don't worry," she said with a smile. "Fortunately, there are a few conversations left for you. And after that, you will come back and wait for the others with me."

"Can I find anyone here?"

"What do you mean?"

"For example, if I go out on the street and knock on the door of a random house, will always be someone in there?"

"Oh no... It would be very nice if this was the case! Unfortunately, you cannot meet new people here. You can only meet those with whom you had real relationship throughout your life."

"So, I can meet my family only?"

"No. You can also meet your neighbors, friends, distant relatives. You can find anyone with whom you had a closer relationship. As I have realized, for seeing someone in the afterlife it is not enough that you came across more than a few times in a week, for example, at the supermarket. It has to be some special kind of relationship, but in the book you cannot read about it."

"When you mentioned the eternal silence, I remembered how good cure for boredom it would be if I could have a chat with anyone here. Not knowing them earlier wouldn't be a problem for me. Meeting new people, with whom we can share our life stories, is much better than silence."

"You want to talk with strangers?"

"Well, if there is no one else, why not?" I answered. "But I was not thinking of complete strangers."

"But who then?"

"I would like to meet celebrities, well-known scientists, musicians, or even historical characters, for instance. Most probably, the system could have been created in a way that we could meet people and celebrities who lived hundreds or thousands years ago. Of course, I am now talking about only those who reached this place, not hell..."

"But sadly, the number of people we can talk with is very limited," my grandmother said.

"Well..." I sighed. "If the only condition to meet

another person is a special kind of relationship during real life, then I will be very lonely here. My relationship with movie stars, for example, was one-sided: only I saw them, only I "knew" them, they did not know anything about me. They did not even suspect that I existed. And this means that I will never meet here celebrities, because I did not have real relationship with them during my life..."

"I agree with you."

"You cannot read in the book anything about this," I continued, "because, according to the original plan, science is not supposed to appear in our lives. However, we might feel that we know a stranger due to modern technology that created film, TV and internet."

"This is true..."

"If I think about it, some people spend more time with a news presenter, for example, than with their family. They see more often the face of a TV star, they hear more often their voice than the voice of their own child, parents, grandparents..."

"It is very sad that most of these people realize it only here in the afterlife," my grandmother said.

"Yes... This is another example how science changes our lives. Indeed it takes away the meaning of it..."

"At the pre-scientific time people used to spend more time with each other. They lived in big and convergent communities, they played with each other and not on computers. Thus, many people had close relationships. Due to this they can meet more people in the afterlife as well, which means that not only our material existence but the life here would also be much enjoyable if science had never appeared."

"This is true," I agreed.

"Imagine how great it would be to meet hundreds of people here. The more souls you can talk with, the more enjoyable the afterlife is. But instead of many people you see only empty houses, just like they were for you during your life, because you did not have any contact with the people who lived there. Or even if you had, it was too shallow."

"Sadly, it is true," I realized. "Many times only a few steps or a wall separates us from our neighbors, from other human beings, but still, we do not know anything about them. It is like they have never existed for us."

"And we cannot change it here, because it is impossible to meet new people. However, it is not the purpose of the afterlife either..."

"Then what is it?" I asked. "Is there something in the book about the function of the afterlife?"

"Yes, there is. According to it, afterlife is nothing else just a rest stop between lives."

"A rest stop?"

"Yes..." my grandmother sighed. "And now listen to

me carefully! The book says that even too much pleasure can be harmful. There is a danger that, if we enjoy life for too long, after a certain period we will be so full of pleasure that later we will never want to live again. However, this system was created in order to be born again and again, in other words, it is a place where we should wait for our next lives impatiently."

"Something very similar happens," I began, "when we eat so much that instead of the pleasant feeling of fullness we have a stomach ache. Or when we eat our favorite food for weeks, for months and after this, we realize that we had enough of it for the rest of our life. We get bored of it for good. And this can be seen in mental activities as well. For instance, it can happen with a good song we have heard so many times that we begin to hate it in the end."

"I agree with you. The only problem is that this book does not state about a candy or a song but about our lives that too much pleasure can be harmful! And this sounds very cynical to us, people from the Earth. Especially to those who suffered a lot..."

"Yes..." I said.

"How would you feel, for example, if you came directly here after your death and if you read that life was so nice and enjoyable that, from time to time, you would need a break in order not to get full of pleasures?"

"I think I would be very confused," I answered.

"My friend, Eve, felt the same at the beginning. But

after some time, the feeling of confusion gave way to disappointment. It is true that she lived for relatively a long time, but her life was not so nice. This is why she decided to give herself another chance: maybe her next life would be somewhat better. And then she had to face the fact that there was no second chance, because the process of rebirth did not work."

"Oh, I am so sorry for her..."

"Before we ran out of our topics and the communication between us became useless, she had kept repeating the following in a bitter voice: *to soak up new experiences, what a lie...*"

"She quoted it from the book, didn't she?"

"Yes. This is the last sentence of the chapter about rebirth. It says: *Go, enjoy life and soak up new experiences!*"

"Well... This sentence really sounds cynical to a person who suffered a lot," I said and I was sure that my grandmother understood: this comment was not related to her friend, Eve, but to me.

"But now, I finally have a reason to meet her again!" my grandmother said happily. "I must tell her that there *is* hope: the Earth is just a bad exception in the Universe."

"I am sure she will feel better."

"Yes. She will be very happy to hear that her next life

will be nice and enjoyable just like our creators imagined it. It will be exactly like it is written in this book. Obviously, we will be reborn only after the mistakes have been corrected by our creators."

"Yes, I think it as well," I said and I remembered immediately the theory of the second creation I had heard about from Yin. I needed to ask my grandmother's opinion, because she was the one, of all those I met after my death, who was the most informed about the afterlife.

– 24 –

"Your eyes have twinkled," my grandmother remarked. "What are you thinking about?" she asked me with a wide smile.

"Well, I have heard a very interesting theory on that other planet, and I liked it very much."

"Tell me quickly!"

"All right," I said. "Let's assume that when our lives end, everyone meets in order to discuss the mistakes we experienced and what we should change. Taking into account everything said, we can create, or more likely, they can create a new body for us. And if needed, even the whole world can be set on a new base. What do you think about it?"

"This theory is very interesting, indeed."

"Yes, I think it as well. The process of rebirth has been suspended and if our creators are to restart it only after the mistakes have been corrected then, in my opinion, the second creation as a solution must have occurred to them as well. Who knows, they might be working on it already.”

“Well, I am not sure...” my grandmother said.

“What is the problem?”

“I have just remembered that I know at least two arguments which suggest that our creators are now dealing with something else. So, I have doubts that they are preparing the second creation.”

“Why do you think so?” I asked in surprise and a little bit disappointed.

“Because of the issue of hell in the first place. It is a huge problem, because many people have been arriving there.”

“You mean that it takes too much time to study everybody’s life individually to find out what they have done? Is this why our creators do not have time to deal with the second creation?”

“No. I think that their biggest problem is the determination of guilt. The Earth must cause a lot of headache to our creators. Much more than you would think at first.”

“How do you know it?”

“In my opinion, it is not easy to deal even with the so-called indisputable points. Of course, we can say that murder is an unforgivable sin. The person who takes away someone’s life should automatically go to hell...”

"I agree with this entirely," I said. "What is the problem then?"

"According to all indications, they really did automate the determination of guilt. At least, its first step."

"I do not understand you."

"Well..." my grandmother began, "I imagine this system as a place where everyone has a digital file. Like a database where every deed is documented, and of course, they can search in it. The system probably works like a software where certain parameters and adequate commands are given. For instance: if someone takes part in a person's loss of life, he should go automatically to hell."

"Is it such a big deal?" I asked still not understanding how serious the problem was.

"Well, it is because judges, who sentenced people to death, are also in hell now. I am speaking about honest and fair people who made the decision that, for example, a child killer should be executed. Such a judge perfectly meets the criteria: he took part in a person's loss of life. And the situation is the same with those policemen who shot down criminals. They also did not reach this place where we are."

"Yes, I see now what you are talking about," I said. "These examples really show that hell is reached automatically—and it is a very big problem. I hope our creators review and consider each case one by one. And if they are now working on this, then I perfectly understand why they do not have time to deal with the second creation."

"I agree with you."

"It is senseless," I continued, "that both the child killer and its judge go to hell. Or both the criminal and the policeman who had shot him. Even the Earth's justice system is fairer than this…"

"Well, I would not say so," my grandmother added. "For instance, your grandfather had been never convicted for mental abuse nor could his case even have reached the court. The world was so different forty years ago..."

"It is true," I nodded.

"His "only" sin was that when he was drunk, he molested his family. He rarely beat us but he constantly kept us in mental terror. For example, he often threatened to kill us. My daughters fell asleep crying, because they were afraid their father would stab them in their dreams. He did not kill anyone, but still, he is in hell."

"So, that certain parameter is obviously not the murder of a person, or the participation in it," I said. "In our creators' eyes the biggest sin must be when we prevent somebody from enjoying life. After all, this was why they had created the human body. And from this point of view the one who "only" ruins somebody's life, is the same as somebody who kills. In both cases the same happens: a person is prevented from enjoying life, feeling good, being happy."

"There might be a point in it," my grandmother admitted. "We have been here for a long time and during our conversations this explanation did not occur to us earlier, because we did not believe what the book claimed: that life consists of pleasure only. But thanks to you this situation has changed..."

"This parameter fits the murderer, the judge by whom he was sentenced to death and the father who made his family suffer," I concluded.

"Yes, you are right, but still, I think that the case of the judge is highly unfair."

"Me too," I said. "I hope that our creators have already realized this problem and taken steps accordingly. I hope that those who have innocently reached hell will not spend much time burning in fire."

"It is not what is happening to them now, I am sure," my grandmother said. "We do not have bodies here, so burning in the fire does not make sense. This penalty would not hurt."

"Of course, I know. I was speaking metaphorically. However, I hope that our creators invented some kind of punishment for bad people."

"Well, only one thing can be here a real punishment: to take away the possibility of rebirth forever."

"Yes, I agree," I said and a terrible thought came to me. "This place, at least now, does not differ from hell in anything, does it? Do I get it right?"

"Sadly, you do," my grandmother answered. "Those people with whom I have talked so far all agree that, due to the fact that the process of rebirth is not functioning now, this place must be exactly like hell. This thought had come to me for a couple of times even before your arrival, but fortunately, you are here now and you have brought hope. The information that the Earth is just a bad exception suggests that the suspension is only temporary."

"So, the people in hell might feel in the same way as your friend, Eve?"

"Yes. They must feel very bad. Imagine how terrible it might be, if after your death a book waited for you saying that you could never live in a body anymore."

"It must be horrible..."

"According to the book, we can be reborn here," my grandmother continued. "It is true that it is not working at the moment, but nothing suggests that it will stay like this forever. Sadly, Eve lost her hope, but I can help her. I will go and tell her all the things I have heard from you."

"Yes, you are free to do it."

"It must be a hellish feeling if you know for sure that you have to stay forever at a place that is so boring and uneventful..."

"I hope that the innocent will be allowed to leave hell shortly," I said. "Our creators must be working on it very hard. It is very important to check every case one by one, since hell is the biggest punishment that a man, a soul can get. The life imprisonment on the Earth is nothing compared to this, because that will end once."

"I agree. But no matter how smart our creators are, this must be a tough task for them. Imagine what would happen if your grandfather had become drunk only once in his lifetime and treated us badly one night only. Obviously, this is not enough for someone to go to hell..."

"Yes, I would also want to know where the limits are. But if one incident is not enough, then how many cases of domestic abuse are necessary for going to hell? Two? Ten? Or at least nineteen?" I asked cynically.

"You are right," my grandmother said. "It is almost impossible to set objective standards."

"And does it matter when the person regrets truly what he has done?" I continued. "If his bad deed caused him so strong twinge of conscience that he could not even sleep well, then his life was also unenjoyable. We can say that he got his punishment even on the Earth. It should be a kind of a mitigating circumstance, right?"

"This is a good question..." my grandmother said.

"And what about the mother who was stealing just to

be able to give food to her child? Will she also be in hell together with the criminal who was stealing from others just to be able to buy drugs?"

"Oh!" my grandmother sighed. "These are very tough questions."

"And can we blame the child who becomes a murderer because of his religious-fanatic parents? He has had no chance to live a different life. And what about those politicians who send their citizens in wars, even if they know that many of them will be killed or seriously injured."

"I do not know how a fair decision could be made..."

"And is it a sin in our creators' eyes if one chooses starvation instead of, for example, robbing others in order to have money for food? Because, by resisting the lure of sin he causes suffering to himself. He deprives somebody—namely, himself—of life enjoyment, and if this really is that certain parameter, then even such a moral person could get to hell."

"I do not want to think about it..."

"But it could happen, right?" I asked. "Did that person take part in making somebody's life impossible to enjoy? Yes, he did. Then he goes to hell!"

"I sincerely hope this is not how the things work..."

"And is an alcoholic guilty," I began my next question, "if he starts drinking because he is not satisfied with his life—that became such due to our creators' mistake? The alcoholic wants only to ease his life with drinking in order to feel better."

"Yes..." my grandmother said. "Ultimately, the responsibility for all is the creators'."

"According to this, should they be in hell as well?" I asked. "Because a lot of people have, had and will have a terrible life on the Earth due to their mistake."

"I do not know what to say... Theoretically, we have a free will. We make our decisions, however, it can happen to anyone that he has to do something bad. For instance, to kill somebody out of self-defense, or to protect the life of somebody else. The people on the Earth constantly get to such situations because of our creators' fault."

"I think," I said, "it is unnecessary to continue talking about this topic, because on the one hand we will just become more moody, and on the other hand it is the creators who will find an adequate solution. I do not think they care what our opinion is."

"Me neither," my grandmother agreed. "Our creators have not communicated with us so far. It is true that this book was written for us, but they did not even note down that the process of rebirth was suspended for a while. They could really refresh the information..."

"I hope they do not have time to deal with it only because they are individually checking everyone who was sent automatically to hell. This can be the only acceptable reason why they do not communicate with us, and why they do not calm us down and inform that the process of rebirth will work again shortly."

"Yes, you are right," my grandmother said and we stopped talking for a time.

"You have said," I began a few seconds later, "that you have two arguments why our creators are not dealing with the second creation at the moment. What is the other one?"

"Well, it is less probable than the theory that they are dealing with hell now. And it does not sound too nice..."

"What is it? Don't hesitate!"

"Well, I can imagine that they do not deal with the second creation, because there is a much easier way to correct their mistake."

"And what is that?" I asked impatiently.

"If in the Universe there is only one planet where something went terribly wrong, isn't it easier to find a solution which refers to that planet only?"

"Well..."

"Is there a need for a completely new creation if the problem is present just on the Earth?"

"This is a good question," I said.

"If a tree's one branch is affected by a disease, then

the first step is not immediately cutting down the whole tree..."

"...but removing the affected branch only," I finished my grandmother's sentence, and sadly, I understood perfectly what her message was.

– 25 –

"Do you believe," I began after the initial shock had passed, "that it is enough to ruin the Earth in order to solve the problem?"

"It would be very surprising if our creators had not thought of this solution. Because if the Earth did not exist, there would be no need for hell."

"But if they had wanted to, they could easily have destroyed the Earth, right?"

"Probably. I do not know whether it is necessary to destroy the whole planet, or just the people who live on it. However, I am sure that the longer our planet exists, the more trouble our creators will have with hell. Thus, the process of rebirth will remain suspended. I am sure that they have not imagined the system in this way..."

"Yes... They might have thought that after designing and creating the world and the human beings, they would relax, get a rest and enjoy the fruit of their work. But instead of that they must be very nervous now..."

"I am sure that the people on the Earth," my grandmother said, "would entirely understand if they all reached this place after a huge catastrophe for example, and heard that our creators could deal with the problem only in this way. Most of them would be even grateful that someone gave them relief, and that now they could be reborn without any risk."

"Risk would still exist," I added. "I have learned that the life on other planets is also not perfect. It is true that there are no wars, diseases and starving children, but the unexpected division of the cells of the organ of the soul is present in every human being in the whole Universe. And it is a huge problem, because after a certain time science also makes life unenjoyable, however, in an entirely different way."

"Then maybe they are not planning the Earth's destruction. They would not achieve anything with it."

"They would one thing though," I said. "They would gain time which is, in my opinion, a crucial factor."

"You are right."

"If they did not need to deal with hell," I continued, "they could cope with the problem that appeared on each planet. And later on, they might even think about the second creation. Because if their aim is to protect us from science appearing in our lives, then they need to create a new human body in which the cells of the organ of the soul are not able to divide. In order to erase our curiosity, a new creation is needed, I am sure."

"Well," my grandmother began, "now I also do not exclude the idea of the second creation, but still, I think it would be a too drastic and maybe even an unnecessary step. After all, the diseased branch cannot only be cut off but it can be healed as well. At least, it is worth trying..."

"Of course, but how do you think they could stop the division of the soul cells? Should they go to every planet and alter everyone's organ of the soul?"

"No, it seems unlikely..."

"The life seeds reached a lot of planets," I continued. "And from then on, in my opinion, our creators cannot influence our physical existence. It is like when we send a probe in the space, and if a physical malfunction happens, we cannot really help. If it is in the Earth's orbit, we might send an astronaut to repair it, but if it has entered outer space, then it is unreachable for us..."

"But the Earth is probably in reachable distance for our creators," my grandmother added. "You said that the reason for all the problems that had appeared only on Earth was that our planet had been too close to the place from where the life seeds had been sent."

"Yes," I said. "But if they wanted to take action, it would have happened already. If it was possible at all."

"What do you mean?"

"I cannot imagine how they could end, for example, wars and crime on the Earth. Division and hatred are such ancient human characteristics that, in my opinion, our creators are powerless. Now it is too late. And if they had not done anything so far, they might have given up..."

“I do not think so,” my grandmother said. “You can see that they have created hell in order to do justice at least here in the afterlife.”

“OK, I have to admit that you are right...”

“So, as I can see, they do care about us.”

“Yes, but I still say that they should not have to deal with hell now, if it was achieved somehow that no one had to go there...”

“Haven’t you said that you could not imagine how this could be realized?”

“Yes, I really do not have any idea...” I sighed. “But…” I began thinking. “This might be achieved, for example, by warning us somehow not to kill, not to steal...”

“Goodness gracious!” my grandmother interrupted me. “This is the Ten Commandments!”

I became speechless and we were just looking at each other for a few seconds. She was smiling, but I was looking at her with my eyes wide opened. I could not say a word in my astonishment.

“They did not give up!” my grandmother broke the silence.

“But are you sure that the Ten Commandments originate from our creators?” I asked skeptically, because I remembered our agreement with Yin and Yang that it was not our creators who had visited the Earth.

“Who else could say such things?” my grandmother asked.

“The members of that traveling civilization who had visited the Earth,” I answered. My grandmother stopped talking and began thinking carefully.

“The Bible,” she began a few seconds later, “is not about a single period of time but it consists of several books which had been written in different eras. So, it could happen that a much more advanced civilization had visited the Earth and settled down, but our creators might have also contacted us. The two are not mutually exclusive.”

“This is true,” I admitted. “It can really happen that the Ten Commandments were sent by our creators, however, I think that the meaning of life and the existence of the afterlife were not revealed by them. By doing so, they would have made our lives less enjoyable. If anyone, our creators are aware of the fact that we mustn’t know about the existence of the afterlife, because otherwise we would not think that life is an only and unrepeatable phenomenon.”

“Still,” my grandmother said, “I think that we might have heard about hell only from our creators. The members of that other civilization who had visited the Earth could not know about the existence of hell. A society devoid of bad people has no reason to suspect or hope that there is a separate place in the afterlife for bad people.”

"You have a point…" I said. "So, do you say that our creators revealed their existence in order to make the Earth a better place?"

"Yes, I do. They needed to tell us there was an afterlife, and what is more, with a separate place for bad people. They might think there was a chance to change us."

"Well..." I sighed. "It is a very good argument that our creators have contacted us or at least, they have sent a message. But I cannot tell that you have convinced me."

"Oh, it is not a problem," my grandmother said smiling. "I have another argument."

"And what is that?"

"It is that we got the Ten Commandments at the dawn of our civilization. Not soon after the first modern people had appeared."

"I see what you mean," I said. "Probably, our creators had been informed even in the beginning that there was a huge problem on the Earth, so they acted immediately. And at that time it was not too late to do something, because hatred and division were not so deep instincts yet. An intervention might have helped then..."

"So, have I already convinced you that our creators contacted us?"

"I think you have," I answered. "I must admit that the

idea of another civilization visiting us in the past cannot explain everything."

"I think so. But it still remains a question why our creators' first intervention did not end with success..."

"You are right..."

"However, the Ten Commandments are a very good guidance to lead a proper life. If everyone lived according to them, hell would be empty."

"I do not know what the problem was," I said. "The messages were clear and understandable, what is more, the possibility of getting to hell had also been mentioned! And still, it did not have much result."

"And their second attempt was not successful either."

"Sorry?" I asked in surprise.

"The style of their second intervention was entirely different: the commanding, threatening tone changed into a kind and loving manner of speech. But unfortunately, the second message was also sent in vain, because it did not change a lot either."

"What are you talking about?"

"Don't you understand who I am talking about?" my grandmother asked with a wise smile.

"No..." I said timidly because, actually, I suspected what her answer would be.

"His mission was to spread love and tolerance. What could be a better answer to division, hatred and wars than the teaching of *love your enemies*? If a stone is thrown at you, throw back some bread in return."

"Jesus?" I asked and I was shocked, because I realized that our creators had undoubtedly intervened and revealed their existence.

"Yes," my grandmother answered. "Only our creators could have sent him. Even the Bible says that he does not originate from this world and that he came to save us."

"To make this planet a better, livable place," I added after my astonishment had gone away.

"Exactly!"

"How did it not occur to me so far… On that other planet I began talking about the Bible, but I did not mention Jesus. I was too sleepy and tired. Also, we concluded that the members of a traveling civilization had contacted us, not our creators. Thus, the last minutes of our conversation took an entirely different line."

"Don't blame yourself!" my grandmother comforted me. "I also did not remember this, even though I have had a number of conversations here. They always took a new direction, if the Bible was ever mentioned."

"But how is this possible?" I asked in a confused way.

"Well… We are now at a place where we should not guess if the stories in the Bible are fictional but we should know the truth."

"Should we?"

"Yes. This is the afterlife, thus, it is very probable that God, or our creators, or whatever we call them, will show up sooner or later. But so far we have not had to appear before anybody, so the only relationship between our creators and us is this book," she pointed towards *The Meaning of Life*. "However, we cannot take it seriously, because there is a huge contradiction between our lives spent on the Earth and what the book says. But now, thanks to you, I understand why it is the case."

"How interesting…" I said. "In a certain sense, the life here is similar to that on the Earth nowadays. In both worlds the only "proof" of our creators' existence is a hardly understandable book full of contradictions. And on the Earth this will not change until we discover the life seeds and the organ of the soul which will serve as a real proof, unlike the Bible..."

"Or until our creators contact us again," my grandmother added.

"Right," I nodded.

"I am so happy that they took action immediately after realizing there was a problem! What is more, they have tried to help us several times, so it is not true at all that they left us alone. They take care of us and this makes me happy and feeling well."

"Yes, grandma, this is right," I began. "But we have to talk about the results as well, or better to say, about the lack of them. I do not want to make you sad, but unfortunately, it is a fact that their interventions did not go well. And let's not talk about the thousands of years old history of mankind. It is enough to think just about the twentieth century. During the cold war the Earth was very close to nuclear destruction. We can call it many things but not in any way a successful intervention. The bitter reality is that, in general, the humanity does not live according to the Ten Commandments and does not follow the teaching of *love your enemies*. Of course, there are exceptions: there will always be people who live according to it, but not many."

My grandmother stopped for a minute to think. Then she said the following:

"In my opinion, the inefficiency is just seemingly the case. Imagine what kind of a place the Earth would be if no one was afraid of punishment. And now I do not talk about hell but the justice system on the Earth that is, in fact, based on the Ten Commandments."

"Well, you are right," I said. "I am taking back my words, or at least, I am modifying them. Because if our creators had not done anything, then probably no one would have a conscience. It is bad even to think about it: a society where no one thinks that bad deeds can have consequences..."

"It would make the Earth an even more terrible place to live."

"I agree. Of course, there would have been people in the history who were not sent by our creators but realized by themselves that the Earth would be a much better place if there were no hatred, murder and crime. However, they would have tried to explain it to others in vain, because no one would have listened. When I speak of this, I mean that, in theory, the chances for success were bigger if the message had been sent by a higher power. And in this sense, their interventions were effective—the message reached a lot of people—but I am sure that this is not only what our creators wanted to achieve. To be more precise, something else was their main goal. This is just a partial result."

"Do you mean that the people still make wars, hate each other, commit crime just like before the Ten Commandments and the arrival of Jesus?"

"Exactly," I answered. "In my opinion, our creators' main goal must be only the complete eradication of these terrible things."

"You are right."

"What is more, Jesus was not the only one. There were similar persons in other religions as well. It is highly probable that our creators have sent more souls to the Earth in order to help. These people were talking about the importance of love, tolerance and peace. Today their followers do the same, however, it does not have much result."

"Then," my grandmother said, "our creators should

try something else, because this method is obviously not adequate to reach their main goal."

"Do you think that they have not given up so far?" I asked.

"Why would they give up? The problem still exists."

"This is true… But I would have given up for sure after the thing that happened with Jesus."

"They did not give up after the Ten Commandments either, however, regarding their main goal it was also an unsuccessful attempt."

"I am not talking about the lack of success," I said. "In my opinion, the reason why our creators stopped trying is not the fact that the teachings of Jesus did not change every person's behavior."

"Then, do you think about the horrible things done in the name of Jesus by many people, among them the church?"

"No," I answered. "But now that you have mentioned it... The inquisition, the wars and the murders in the name of Jesus and God are also adequate to discourage our creators from additional attempts."

"But what are you talking about then?"

"About the crucifixion," I said and I sighed. "How would you feel in our creators' place? They had sent Jesus on the Earth to spread love, but they had to face the fact that we executed him mercilessly. This was our response to their attempt of making Earth a better place. Can you imagine something more disappointing for our creators?”

My grandmother did not say a word. I could not decide whether she was speechless because she was waiting for me to continue, or because she was still thinking about what she has heard.

“Wouldn’t you think that after this it is unnecessary to do anything?” I continued. “I, for example, would think that the situation is hopeless. What kind of message does it send to our creators that we killed the person who had been sent here to spread love and tolerance? What might they think of us?”

After my questions we both remained silent. The next one was asked by my grandmother:

“What if the humanity runs towards their end according to a plan?”

“What do you mean?”

“What if our creators’ latest—and at the same time last—intervention is that they will not do anything?”

“Willingly?”

“Yes,” she answered. “And if this is the case, then you are right that they had left us alone, and strangely, I am also right when I claim that they care about us.”

“This sounds really strange.”

"But it is logical. In the beginning, thousands of years ago, our creators might have thought they could change something. So they sent the Ten Commandments and Jesus. But by now, they must have realized that the best would be if they just let us destroy ourselves. After all, the problem would be solved: no one could be born on the Earth anymore. Sooner or later our planet will become uninhabitable due to a nuclear war, or because we will clear the forests, pollute the air and the water, cause enormous changes in the weather."

"I think you are right," I said. "Now I remembered the story of Noah's Ark. There is no point thinking that it is only a fictitious story, so this means that our creators have intervened at least once in the past. And at that time, *they* had to take action due to our low level of science. We could not destroy our planet then, but nowadays we are able to do that."

"This is right. So, our creators only have to leave us alone..."

"Well, grandma, a few minutes earlier you could hardly imagine that they have given up," I remembered. "But now you think the same."

"If only I did not need to think it," she sighed. "If only!"

– 26 –

"Has the eternal silence already begun?" I asked because this time we have been silent for ten or fifteen seconds, not only for two or three.

"No, this is only an awkward silence," my grandmother answered with irony in her voice.

"Then everything is all right!" I replied with a smile on my face and feeling of relief, which caused my grandmother's bad mood to disappear immediately.

"It is true that there are fewer and fewer topics," she said with a smile, "but fortunately, there is still one we have not mentioned. We have not talked about what's new at home, what happened to you and the family after I had left."

"We really have not..." I said and I became sad again, because I knew this conversation would not last for long.

"Where did your smile disappear?" my grandmother noticed.

"The problem is that I cannot tell you much," I began. "As I have said already, I became sick six months after your death. I went to the hospital immediately, and I stayed there until my last day. So, I can tell you only about the things that had happened to the family before my hospital treatment began, but there is not much to say…"

"Nothing happened?"

"Well, after I have learned what the meaning of life is," I sighed and looked at the book lying on the table, "it is very hard to say out loud, but sadly, nothing did happen. Our life was uneventful after your death. Of course, we tried to get over the grief quickly: we always told each other that you would be very sad if you saw us. We believed you would like if we did not cry so much, if we continued our lives and if we were happy..."

"Of course I would like that," my grandmother added.

"Yes, we were sure about this. But you know it very well that mourning lasts for very long, especially if the death of a loved one happens unexpectedly. We did not suspect at all that you would die that day."

"Neither did I..."

"I have heard on the other planet that, according to the original plan, everyone should die in the way you did. But still, I think that the unexpected leaving makes the mourning even more painful. I know that it is a selfish idea, but the relatives can more easily accept the death of their loved one if he was suffering a lot previously. Of course, I do not wish you had a fatal disease and were suffering for months, but it is sure that if it had been the case, your death would have been a relief for us too. We would have thought it was better for all of us, because everyone's suffering ended."

"I see what you are talking about. You are right."

"So, the first months were spent in mourning. I remember that immediately after your death, every time there was a strange noise, or even when the bulb burned out, we believed you were in the house. I wanted so much to get a message from you somehow."

"In such cases it is normal," my grandmother comforted me with a smile.

"And when the mourning began to pass away and it seemed that life would be the same as it had been previously, the depressing news arrived that a good friend of mine had also died. And after it the real tragedy happened: it turned out that I had a fatal disease. But I will stop now, because you asked me even in the beginning not to talk about this."

"Yes, it is entirely unnecessary..."

"So, at this moment the family is in mourning again, but now because of *my* death," I said and remembered immediately my parents and brother. "Oh, my God... Poor them! I realize only now how sad they must be... I am ashamed of myself that I did not remember them at all. But so many things happened after my death…" I referred to my involuntary visit at Yin and Yang's planet.

"Don't feel bad! It is also normal. When people arrive

to the afterlife and meet one of their deceased loved ones, they usually do not think about what their loved ones might be doing on the Earth at the moment."

"I think I know exactly what they are doing at the moment," I said. "First of all, they must have found a relief, because they do not need to watch me suffering anymore. I saw them for the last time yesterday, when they visited me in the hospital. We agreed we would meet again tomorrow... I do not know whether they were serious, but I was almost sure that I could not bear another day. However, the worst was that I had to act every time as though I did not realize they were trying to hide their tears..."

Then my grandmother took my hand which, sadly, I could not feel. She was smiling, but her eyes were sad.

"But now," I continued, "they can cry. You passed away a year ago, I passed away today. It might be too much for them. I am not sure whether they can get over it. Oh, my God, how sad it would be if their lives were ruined because of this..."

"Don't be sad!" my grandmother calmed me. "We cannot do anything just hope that they would again remember the only argument that can help in such cases: you would not like if your death messed up their lives."

"You see, this is why it would be so good to be able to send them a message from here."

"And what would you say?"

"First of all, I would calm them down that they did not need to worry, because I had arrived to a very good and nice place. They do not need to know how boring and uneventful it is comparing to the material world. I am sure they would forgive me this white lie."

"Me too," my grandmother said smiling.

"And my main message would be to enjoy life at most, to soak up as much experience as they can, so when the time comes, we will have much to talk about. They told me on the other planet that our lives would lose their meaning if we knew what it was and that the afterlife existed. But still, I think that it would help a lot the people at home, if we could contact them. To say a sentence, at least."

"I agree with you," my grandmother began. "But sadly, we cannot contact them. I would also like them to come here many-many years later with a lot of stories. It is easy to be smart now, but it is such a great pity if our real lives become as uneventful and boring as they will be in the afterlife. It is a huge mistake if we do not enjoy life as much as we can, even in hard times. We have to grab every opportunity to gain new experiences with our loved ones. It is true that, for example, we can play cards here, but it is not so enjoyable and precious pastime as it was in our lifetime..."

"So, nothing remains but the hope that they will take our advice, even if they cannot hear us now."

"I know they will," my grandmother said with a

soothing smile. And because it seemed she was serious, I also calmed down.

"I think that this topic has come to its end." I said. "Can the eternal silence begin now?"

"Fortunately, it is still away. It is coming, but we will have other stories to talk about. We have many nice memories and it will be good to recall them. And also, you have to meet the others. While you are away to find your recently deceased friend for example, I will not be bored either, because I must visit Eve."

"Oh, yes, to tell her the good news."

"Right!" my grandmother nodded. "She will be happy if she knows that, originally, a much better life was meant for us, and that the next one will be perfect for sure. And I will inform others as well, not just Eve. Let the whole afterlife know!"

"But how could everyone hear it?" I asked in surprise. "We can only meet a few people here."

"You don't need to worry. The new information travels far and very fast here. I will let four or five persons know, who will tell it to other four or five persons and they will also spread the news among their acquaintances, relatives. In the end, everyone will know the great news you have brought. Even people whose existence we do not know anything about."

"This is great!" I said enthusiastically. "According to this, the experiment was not in vain. Of course, from the point of view of the two scientists I met on the other planet it was, but now it helps us a lot: the facts I have heard from them explain everything."

"Did they make an experiment with you?" my grandmother asked. "You have not told me it so far."

"You are right," I said. "I became a subject of an experiment despite my will. They made it in order to get to know, even before their own death, what kind of place the afterlife is by using the souls of deceased people. This is why I was stopped on my journey to the afterlife. Their plan was that they would bring me back from here, after a certain time, in order to inform them where I had been and what I had learnt."

"Does it mean that you will disappear shortly?"

"I do not think so, because they have never succeeded so far. Not one soul could they bring back."

"Well, it is not surprising at all, since the process of rebirth is suspended," my grandmother concluded.

"Now, that you have mentioned it..." I began thinking. "Yes, this might be the reason why they cannot bring back anybody from here. Our creators do not let any soul leave this place."

"Thus, they are trying in vain."

"Well, yes... And the strangest thing is that they make this experiment firstly in order to know whether we can live in bodies again after death. They do not even suspect that each of their attempts might fail, because no one can be reborn at the moment. Their continuous failure is actually the answer..." I explained but judging by my grandmother's gaze, her thoughts were already somewhere else. Thus, I got up from the couch and I said the following: "I think we can go now."

"All right, let's go," she agreed and stood up as well. I became sad which my grandmother realized immediately. "What is the problem now?" she asked.

"Nothing," I answered. "It is a little strange that we only met a few hours ago, but we have to separate again."

"There is nothing strange in it. Sooner or later everyone visits their deceased relatives and friends. What is more, it will be useful because in a few hours, when we will meet again, we will have topics to talk about," she said and we headed towards the front door.

"This is true," I nodded. "I would also like to know how Eve will react to the good news."

"It will turn out soon," she said enthusiastically and we stepped out of the house. "It is very important that everyone gets the good news. You have spent too little time here to understand how much the information you have brought will help the hopeless people here."

"I think I can imagine it," I said.

"Where does your friend live?" she asked when we arrived to the gate.

"Over there," I pointed to the right side.

"All right. Then our ways separate," she said because Eve's house was in the other direction. "But we will meet soon at the same place. I mean, not in front of the gate, of course, but in the house," she added laughing.

"OK" I said with a smile on my face.

My grandmother hugged me and we said goodbye.

I began to go towards the house of my recently deceased friend on this beautiful spring morning. It did not surprise me at all that the sun was still standing as low as when I had arrived a few hours ago.

And even though I missed the pleasant warmth of the sun rays on my face, the smell of the spring flowers and the soft breeze, I was happy. First of all, because I found out that my grandmother was also blissful. When I had arrived, she could not hide her sadness due to my early death, and I always had a slight twinge of conscience because of it. But fortunately, this feeling went away at the moment of our separation.

After this, only one thing could cause me a twinge of conscience: if I remembered that one day my loved ones would also get here, and when I would ask them what happened after I had passed away, their answer would be *Nothing* due to my tragic death.

As my grandmother had said, it would be such a great pity.

Made in the USA
San Bernardino, CA
02 December 2019